If I'd been in a Falcon when I left Rat Johnson's rock, the Patrol wouldn't have got in the lucky shot that crippled me. Not having had a Falcon to run in, I maybe should have surrendered when I knew I was sighted; if I'd had any sense, I probably would have. The battered old Company Ford I flew was never meant for smuggling. I had already off-loaded Rat Johnson's supplies, and his was the last illegal delivery on my schedule. The most the Patrol could have proved against me, once I left his rock, was that I was off my assigned course by a considerable margin.

However, one thing I've seldom been accused of is having any sense.

SKYRIDER

1

SKIRMISH

SKYRIDER

1

SKIRMISH

MELISA C. MICHAELS

TOR

A TOM DOHERTY ASSOCIATES BOOK

SKIRMISH

Copyright © 1985 by Melisa C. Michaels

The prologue originally appeared as part of a short story, "I Have a Winter Reason," published in the March 16, 1981, issue of *Isaac Asimov's Science Fiction Magazine,* copyright © 1981 by Davis Publications, Inc.

First printing: March 1985

A TOR Book

Published by Tom Doherty Associates
8-10 West 36 Street
New York, N.Y. 10018

Cover art by Bruce Jensen

ISBN: 0-812-54566-4
CAN. ED.: 0-812-54567-2

Printed in the United States of America

For "Mama Cookshack,"
because I said I would;
and for M.V.W., because.

Skyrider 1

SKIRMISH

PROLOGUE

There are ghosts among the asteroids. Ghosts of warriors and workers, ghosts of pilots and passengers, and ghosts of the Gypsies who originally settled the Belt. The Gypsies speak in ancient Romani, and ask nothing of anyone but that they be left to their dreams.

I never heard them before the accident. I never had nightmares before, either. Nor a metal plate in my head to hold my brains in. At first I wondered whether that had anything to do with it, with the ghosts and the nightmares. But when I asked the med-techs, they muttered polysyllabically about survivor guilt, said I should feel grateful my pretty face wasn't marred, and suggested I might be due for a vacation.

I'd read about survivor guilt. My cousin Michael was a warrior in the Colonial Incident. His sister was killed in the Battle of Viking Plain. His first wife

Maria was a member of the Lost Platoon. If anyone had a right to survivor guilt, it was Michael. And he mentioned occasional nightmares, but no ghosts. He made a good living on Mars and had a life as secure and prosaic and safe as any good Earther could dream of. And it seemed to me that if an ex-warrior could make a life for himself, the survivor of a stupid accident like mine should, too.

I took a passenger shuttle out and damn near crashed it when I heard the Gypsies singing. My payload never knew how close it was, but I did. I decided maybe the psych-tenders were right. Maybe I could use a vacation.

The reunion wasn't really planned; it just happened. I knew Michael would be coming to Earth, but I probably wouldn't have made the trip if I'd had any idea how many Earth-based Rendells were going to show up. The inevitable culture shock of coming Earthside was bad enough, without the added nerve-wracking knowledge that there were so many related Earthers watching to see what bizarre and unacceptable character traits I might have picked up in twenty years in the Belt.

My first day planetside, it rained. Water, huge drops of it, fell right out of the sky. Out of thunderclouds piled like towering wads of dirty air-filter material overhead. Sky was a concept I'd got myself ready for, before I planeted. Water falling out of it was something else again.

Then there was the air. Limitless breathable air, unchambered, unguarded; and it *moved*. It took me two full days to get over the feeling, every time I stepped out of a dwelling, that my chamber had blown a giant leak and I should dive for a space suit. I could have accepted a gentle breeze; in large chambers the air does move, sometimes enough that you can feel it. But not briskly. When air moves briskly, people had better move briskly, too, if they want to go on breathing.

While I was getting used to air that moved briskly and to water that fell out of the sky, indigenous life forms bit me. They left little red welts that swelled and itched. Mosquitoes, gnats, flies. . . . None of this was entirely new, of course. I did live Earthside the first ten years of my life. But in twenty years gone, I'd forgot what to expect of a planet. Not all the rediscovery was fun.

Even the temperature wasn't properly regulated. I suppose I should amend that statement; I've put it in terms of the asteroids. On Earth, God regulates the temperature, and mostly what She does is assumed to be for the best. But in the area of temperature control I thought She did a lousy job.

After four days Earthside I was still too uncomfortable to do much of anything at midday but sip soy beer in the shade with Michael. We sat at a picnic table under a tree while all the Earthers were inside eating lunch. God regulates the temperature on Mars, too (with a little help from the Terraformers), but on Mars She keeps the heat to a reasonable minimum. Michael didn't seem any more comfortable in the broiling sun of Earth than I.

I couldn't think of anything to talk to him about. I kept tilting my head back every once in a while to get a look at the puffy white clouds that dotted the deep blue sky. I didn't like to look at it too long. It made my eyes dizzy.

"Penny for your thoughts," said Michael.

He'd grown man-size and then some in the twenty years since I'd last seen him. Somehow I hadn't expected that; nor the serious, intent way he looked at people; nor the sudden, stunning beauty of his rare smile. When we were children, I thought he was plain. A redheaded, freckle-faced monster, good for nothing but tormenting girl-cousins.

"What's a penny?" I asked. "I've always wondered."

He shrugged, a gesture I was aware of, though I didn't turn to look at him. There was something about the way those eyes watched me. . . . I wouldn't look. "It was a U.S. coin," he said. "Prob'ly worth a fortune as a collectible by now, so I hope you don't accept the offer."

There were hints of the red-haired boy in his mannerisms, but not in the dark of his eyes. "I was thinking," I said, watching him, "how many rules there are to follow on Earth."

The shadowed eyes widened almost imperceptibly. His face was lean and vulnerable, devoid of freckles. "Rules?"

I looked back at the sky. It hurt my eyes, but not as much as looking at him. "You know," I said. "Social rules. Acceptable behavior."

I wasn't really sure he did know. Mars was more similar to Earth than to the asteroid belt. He might be perfectly comfortable here. Even the environment

was more familiar to him than to me. He was used to
sky, and clouds, and all-day gravity, and houses, and
the whole long list of everything physical that made
this so different from the asteroids. All the things that
made me uncomfortable, perpetually on edge, alert
on a subliminal level because things were so uncon-
trolled, so gut-level *wrong*. I stared at Michael over
the top of my beer, waiting.

He met my gaze without blinking. "It's not really
very important," he said. "If you don't know a
rule—"

"They'll crow over it. You were going to say
they'd excuse me because I'm from the Belt, right?
Well, wrong. Haven't you seen the cat-faced old
ones watching? Didn't you see the way they eyed my
table manners and hung on every casual word I spoke
at dinner last night? Aunt Hazel and Uncle Alfred
and Grandma Rendell—they're just waiting to pounce."

He studied me. I wanted to look away, but didn't.
"Sounds paranoid," he said.

It reminded me of the psych-tenders, and I grinned.
"Even paranoids have enemies. Some people hate
us."

Something dark, like a shadow from the sun, crossed
his eyes. "Not hate," he said with startling certainty.

I stared. "Course not. Was a joke." Then I remembered, and frowned. "Oh. I've read that before, from
veterans of the Incident. Loaded word?"

He hesitated. "I guess I have a lot of them.
'Incident' is another."

"Sorry. I know they called it a war on Mars."

His eyes went so dark inside themselves I couldn't

13

look at them. "It *was* a war. You weren't there; you don't—"

"I know. Nobody who wasn't there gets to talk about it. I've read *that* before, too. So space it, okay?" Suddenly unaccountably sad, I gulped down half my beer before turning back to the sky.

"Sorry," he said.

I ignored him. I hadn't realized before I planeted how *big* a sky would be. I wasn't nearly accustomed to it yet. Staring into the bottomless blue, I thought suddenly, *If the gravity generator fails now* . . .

Startled, I clutched the table, and forcibly reminded myself of the laws of physics. The Earth itself was the gravity generator here, and that couldn't fail.

"You can't handle sky, can you?"

His voice surprised me. In my moment of private terror I'd nearly forgot his presence. But with his words, the world fell back into place and I heard again the moving air in the deciduous tree overhead and the discordant jangle of birdsongs in the distance. "I can handle *any*thing," I said with undue ferocity, and lifted my beer.

"Even rules?"

I put the beer down and stared at him. I really didn't know who he was. I never heard this voice in his letters. We corresponded on printout chips, not voice; but I'd imagined that the voice that typed the words he sent would sound different from this. . . . This was a total stranger. My cousin Michael. "If I have to. Even rules," I said carefully.

He grinned in triumph. It lighted his whole face till even the darkest shadows of his eyes were banished and I saw, just for a moment before the smile faded, the face of the freckled child I knew. "Gotcha," he said.

I couldn't return the smile. I was living on nerves alone, and they were badly jangled. The air kept moving; the indigenous life forms kept biting and singing; and the sky was painfully blue, with a sun in it so near and so hot I found it hard to understand how this planet ever came to be settled in the first place. The fact that our ancestors evolved here was irrelevant. It was a hostile environment.

And now I saw a gaggle of elders emerging from the house, sloe-eyed and content from their meal. I couldn't face them. I could not, at that moment, tolerate their eyes—or their rules—or my cousin Michael, the stranger. "I'm going for a walk." I rose without waiting for a reply. The elders, and Michael too, could make of it what they would; I didn't really care if it was bad form to walk away from them. I walked.

I wanted to cry. I'd had too much beer—far more than I was used to—and I was turning into a weepy drunk. There's probably something more tiresome than a weepy drunk, but I couldn't think just then what it would be.

The Rendell residence—my mother's white clap-board home—was right on the edge of town, and I headed out for the dark green fields where nobody would stare at a misplaced Belter. Which is how I found myself walking past the rusting wrought-iron fence of a cemetery after a while.

I'd forgotten cemeteries. It took a moment for the

full significance of the white crosses and colored granite blocks to sink in. Earthers buried their dead whole—or at least those dead whose parts weren't reusable or whose relatives chose not to permit their reuse.

I paused outside the gate, waiting to hear the Gypsies. Afraid to hear the Gypsies. Maybe afraid I wouldn't hear the Gypsies. I closed my eyes, and opened them again abruptly when what I saw on the inside of my eyelids was the reflection of Django's smile.

But Django wasn't here. He was somewhere lost in the Belt, floating and singing, singing. . . .

Inside the gate, the first gravestone I came to was inscribed in bold stone-cut letters: ELLIOT REN-DELL—BORN 1924—KILLED IN ACTION 1944. I paused, staring, barely aware of the breeze that bent the tallest weeds. Elliot Rendell. A relative? Some multi-great-uncle or cousin?

A nearby bird burst into joyous song just as I bent to touch the sun-warmed stone: and my fingers sank deep into the unforgiving past, caught on memories not my own:

The chatter of an automatic weapon. The shrill death-voice of mortar fire. The screams, the pitiful howling cries and the tangy dark scent of blood and scattered earth. . . . A sense of fear. A sense of failure. A sense of overwhelming loss. . . . There were vultures raucous in the hard blue sky. There were shadows converging; there were the screams of the damned and the dying, and the salt taste of tears in my mouth; and through it all the fierce longing like unappeasable hunger—PLEASE GOD I WANT—

With a startled whimper I jerked my fingers away from the stone and fell back into here-and-now with a rush that left me dizzy. The sky stretched forever above my head. Below my head? I choked on a scream and threw myself full-length in the dusty ground cover, fingers clawing for some safe purchase in the moist black earth beneath, and inadvertently I touched another stone.

REBECCA GARDENER RENDELL, it said. 1966–2054.

There were pretty red roses as sweet and deep and perfect as God could make them. Very carefully she pricked out their image with needle and thread on the hem of the little dress, and thought with whimsical regret how much sweeter if the stitched ones could be scented as God's were. . . . A rocking chair empty in a shaft of dusty sunlight. . . . A browned and cracking photograph whose image muddled and disappeared behind tears. . . . White curtains that shifted and blew in a morning breeze heavy with sunlight and birdsong. . . . And a delicate whisper, gentle and infinitely sad: Please God I want . . .

I pulled my hand away, but it was too late. I could hear them all now, their voices raised in discordant melancholy, their images like mirrors fractured in the sun:

pleasegodiwant . . .

"I'm sorry," I said. I didn't mean to say it. The words popped out of their own accord, and they wouldn't stop. "I'm sorry, I'm sorry, I'msorryI'm-sorry . . ." It mingled with the voices of the dead: "I'm sorry please God I want I'm sorry please God I want I'msorrypleaseGodIwant . . ."

When I realized the end of both sentences, theirs and mine, was ". . . to be alive," I shut up. My head hurt. I realized I was holding it, crouched in the sun-scented ground cover with both hands folded over the top of my head where under the scalp there was a metal plate to hold me together; and I let go and sat up.

The voices seemed quieter. There was still a prism effect of memories pushing and shoving at one another for space in my mind, but none of them were mine. None except Django, and he wasn't even here. He was somewhere in the asteroids, lost and dead because of a stupid accident that never should have happened; and I was here in green ground cover and yellow sunlight, listening to ghosts that weren't real.

"Melacha?"

Michael's voice. It startled me. I turned and saw him watching me from the graveyard gate.

"Melacha, are you all right?"

I was still half caught in the memories. "Can you hear them?" I wasn't even vaguely aware how the question might sound if he *couldn't* hear them.

He hesitated, then passed the gate and walked with long, sure strides across the ground cover toward me. "I can hear them." There was a look in his eyes I didn't understand. He sat on the ground cover beside me. "What happened?"

I stared. "When?"

"Whatever it was you didn't send me a chip about.

18

Whatever it was that sent you running for Earth. Whatever it was that made you come out to the cemetery to listen to ghosts.''

"He wasn't ready to die," I said, as if in answer.

"Nobody's ready to die. Haven't you been listening? Look at the dates on these stones. It doesn't matter if somebody lives two years or two hundred, death always comes too soon."

"It was so stupid."

"There's no smart way to die. Tell me, Melacha."

I told him. I didn't know how much he knew about shuttles or about the asteroids or about air filters, but I told him the whole pathetic, foolish story. The accident that could have happened in anybody's living room, only it happened on my shuttle and it killed my lover. And it was my fault. And you don't get a second chance, in space.

We had to make two docking procedures. People die every day in docking procedures, but we didn't.

We had to duck an unexpected flurry of "wild" rocks. People die every day in evasive actions, but we didn't.

Django had survived, in his life, two holed chambers and two Insurrectionist battles. He had survived the rescue mission that brought the *Sunjammer* in at the cost of three people's lives. He had survived the *Big Eagle*'s fiasco flight. He died on my shuttle of a clogged air filter that blew its top because I didn't check the tubes before the flight.

It was no particular comfort that I damn near died with him. "Damn near" is the operative phrase there. If I had died, I'd be out there singing with the

Gypsies. But I didn't. I survived, and Django died. In just about the stupidest, most useless way any Belter ever did die, short of walking out of a chamber without a suit.

Michael listened without comment, all the way through to the end. Then he said, watching me, "People die every day."

I didn't look at him. "Why did you come out here?"

"Out where?"

"To the cemetery."

"I thought you might need me."

I looked at him, but there were no answers in those shadowed eyes. "So you could tell me people die?" I was startled at the bitter sound of my voice.

To my surprise, he smiled. "Partly that."

"And?"

"And to hold your hand. And to let you know you aren't alone. Other people listen to the ghosts. Everybody's guilty."

"Other people's ghosts are real."

"No more real than yours. You have a right to your pain, Melacha. But you have a right to your life, as well. It's okay for you to be alive."

"You came out here to tell me *that?*" But that was enough. It was the first step on a long road back to reason and sense: the gift of acceptance.

I never did get used to living under a sky. I'm more comfortable in the asteroids, where life is carefully bounded by stone and steel and plastic and I know what the boundaries are and how to behave.

But I learned to pilot a shuttle again, safely among

the songs of Gypsies not everyone can hear. Sometimes I sing with them. And when I'm dead, I'll join them.

But not yet.

CHAPTER ONE

Half the warning lights in the cockpit were blinking at me when I got back to Home Base, and most of the others were burned out. None of the controls responded properly, though they weren't all dead. My head hurt. I put one hand flat on top of it in what I knew had become a characteristic gesture, absently testing for some outward evidence of the metal plate inside. All the surgeons had left was a thin three-cornered scar, invisible under my hair. They'd been more concerned about my appearance than I was.

The klaxon that warned of a failing synch system sounded abruptly, shattering the silence around me. I shut it off. The people who designed the shuttles we flew should have to fly them. What the hell use was a klaxon that warned of something we couldn't do a damn thing about?

But I knew the logic. Without a synch system, one could presumably not catch and match an asteroid. If one couldn't catch and match, one ditched. Obviously.

I had no intention of ditching. I was carrying Company cargo, and I didn't intend to lose it, or even to share its value with a salvage crew. I couldn't afford that. I was saving up for a shuttle worth flying.

If I'd been in a Falcon when I left Rat Johnson's rock, the Patrol wouldn't have got in the lucky shot that crippled me. Not having had a Falcon to run in, I maybe should have surrendered when I knew I was sighted; if I'd had any sense, I probably would have. The battered old Company Ford I flew was never meant for smuggling. I had already off-loaded Rat Johnson's supplies, and his was the last illegal delivery on my schedule. The most the Patrol could have proved against me, once I left his rock, was that I was off my assigned course by a considerable margin.

However, one thing I've seldom been accused of is having any sense. I didn't surrender. I don't take kindly to being arrested, even if I'm let go later for lack of evidence. That sort of thing can play hell with a smuggler's reputation. I turned tail and ran before they knew what they were chasing. If I never had to explain what I'd been doing in that sector, the Patrol would have that much less excuse to keep an eye on me. They certainly didn't need more than they already had.

Typical of the Earther mentality that governs the Patrol, they took a couple of potshots at me, even though they weren't near enough to scan my identity.

Earthers didn't give a damn. They couldn't scan what I was, but they could scan what I wasn't: my image wouldn't come close to anything Earth-based, and I wasn't half sleek or swift enough to be carrying any important (read "Earther") Company personnel. The best guess was that I was a long-haul cargo shuttle, and the location meant I was probably not on a Company run. That was all the Patrol needed to know.

They would never have given up so easily if they'd known they hit me. Gut shot, my shuttle handled a lot like a freefalling rock. But I did lose the Patrol, and after that all I had to do was nurse my bleeding rattletrap Ford halfway across the Belt, through most of the "wild" rocks anybody ever heard of. Which was why I was there in the first place. There were a lot of smugglers in the Belt, but not many who would make a run for Rat Johnson. Most of them had plans for the future that did not include dying for the sake of a wrinkled little beady-eyed Romany freelancer who'd been on his chosen rock longer than most of us had been alive and who still couldn't usually save up enough malite between runs to pay for the supplies he ordered. There were plenty of freelancers who could pay, and most of them mined rocks a lot easier to catch and match than Rat's. Most of them were not surrounded by wild rocks, and all the others I knew of had synch systems. Nobody ever said smuggling would be easy, but one wanted a chance at survival. And it was expected to turn a tidy profit; ostensibly, that was why we did it. But it was more than Rat could offer.

Still, I liked him. He was a crazy old man with a dream. And hell, dodging wild rocks was good practice. Same as catching and matching odd little tumblers with no synch systems. It kept me on my toes. Besides, I'd been buying Rat's supplies for years. I couldn't quit now. He'd become an investment. If he ever did strike the vein of malite he swore that little rock was hiding, we'd both be rich. Unless I let the Patrol shoot my shuttle out from under me, Company cargo and all, on a routine run.

I nursed the Ford home by inches, watching warning lights blink on and burn out all the way. And not once did I hear any Gypsies. I don't know why. Usually they sang. And I was listening for them. Especially after my head started to hurt. But I didn't hear them.

When I finally limped into range of Home Base, I forgot to listen anymore. I was concentrating on what was left of my controls. My synch system was dying, but it wasn't dead yet. I had a chance . . . until a bright little short-run shuttle slid in ahead of me to synch up for landing.

There was a brief chatter of static from the Comm Link when I turned it on. "Who the hell do you think you are, rock jockey?" I asked the short-runner. "Get the hell out of my space before I knock you out of it!" I was as low on fuel as I was on patience, but I hit the jockey thrusters anyway, angling for position.

The little short-runner dodged like a scared Earther, but the pilot knew how to curse. When he got done showing off his vocabulary, he added somewhat more politely, "Who the hell I think I am is a Company pilot, same like you, hotshot. And in case you didn't notice, I got here first. So why don't you just lug that heap of tin out of my way and shut up about it?''

I tried to edge him out, but he was too quick for my crippled Ford. ''I'll ram that variegated little rock-hopper down your throat,'' I said, though it must have been as evident to him as it was to me that I couldn't even get near him. The pilot's voice was unfamiliar; probably one of the new short-runners hired while I was Earthside nursing my grief and self-pity after Django died.

The Comm Link chattered more static at me. ''Ah, this is Flight Control,'' it said placatingly. ''Skyrider, ah, that is, shuttle Alpha Three Seven, please hold your position. Jamin's on an emergency Sick Bay run. Ah, shuttle Zed Eight Four Three Five, you have clearance. We have an ambulance waiting. I repeat, you are cleared for landing. Engage synch system please.''

I could have claimed right of way. My systems malfunctions warranted that, even over a Sick Bay payload. I could have made him wait while I limped in past him. But Flight Control obviously didn't have me on scan yet, or Granger would have ordered me in. I figured a few more minutes wouldn't kill me. Anyway, I hoped they wouldn't. I said, ''Holding,'' and another warning light blinked on over the failing synch system controls. I ignored it.

The great Skyrider. Hotshot pilot. Risk taker. Law-breaker. I'd have been wiser to stick to breaking the artificial laws Humankind imposed on the world. Now I was meddling with the laws of physics, and

those are a good deal harder to break with impunity.
I expect God has Her reasons. I know She doesn't
often give outright idiots a second chance. But that
"hotshot" business rankled. All the more since it
was a word I'd been known to use, myself. Referring
to myself. That was fine for me, but it didn't give a
short-runner the right to use it in that mocking tone.

I told myself that if Jamin had been carrying an
ordinary payload, I'd have demanded my right of
way and to hell with him. I tell myself a lot of things
like that. Lies, to put it nicely. The plain fact was
that he'd called me "hotshot," and I, in a fit of
adolescent rage, had decided to show him what a real
hotshot could do.

I never could resist a challenge.

The Comm Link chattered static. I turned off the
transmitter and stared at Home Base. "Hell, I could
land this crate on a pebble." My voice cracked on
the last syllable, when another warning klaxon startled me. I had to flip three switches to get it turned
off. "I'll damn well show him, even if the whole
synch system goes out while I'm waiting for him to
get his pretty little short-runner down."

The synch system went out, leaving behind a new
rash of warning lights and the foul odor of burnt
electronics.

"And afterward," I said evenly, "I'll kill that
space-happy son of a bitch."

"Ah, Alpha Three Seven, ah, please say again?"

"I said I'll—oh." I stared at the control board;
Granger shouldn't have heard that. But one of the
many new warning lights was over the Comm Link. I

cleared my throat. "That is, how's my signal? D'you have me on scan yet?" If I couldn't turn it off, I might as well use it. "Most of my controls are malfunctioning; I ran into some wild rocks the other side of New England."

Shuttle Z8435, the pretty little rock-hopper that had claimed my space, floated down onto the flight deck while Granger scanned my damage. When I heard him whistle, I knew I was in trouble. But I'd known that already. His voice was businesslike as he cleared the flight deck and ordered Fire Control and Damage crews to stand by. Then he hesitated, and his concern wasn't quite so well hidden when he spoke again. "Skyrider, I've seen junked shuttles in better condition than that. You sure you want to ride it in?"

Jamin cut in before I could answer. I could just make out the bright yellow ambulance off-loading his passengers. "I scan burn damage, hotshot. How in space did an uncharted asteroid do that?"

Granger and I answered simultaneously. He said, "Not on the Comm Link, Jamin," while I said, "Space it, rock jockey." Granger's was probably the more telling remark; however ignorant Jamin was, he had to know the Comm Link was frequently monitored for just that sort of revealing exchange. And unless he had something personal against me, why would he want to get me arrested? Not just for angling for landing space, surely. Not unless he really was an Earther. Or an honest-to-God Company man. Which apparently he wasn't, since he did shut up.

The interruption had served one good purpose; Granger had forgot his own question. I didn't have to justify my intent to ride that wreck home. Which was just as well. I couldn't have come up with a rational answer if he'd asked again. But all he said was, "Good luck, Skyrider."

I could use it. Without my synch system, which should operate in tandem with the flight deck computer, I would have to land on manual. Same as on Rat Johnson's rock, only there I had a fully operational shuttle to work with. And a sweet old beady-eyed Gypsy who depended on me to make it.

Not that I'd have admitted the importance of that; it was his malite I wanted, and that was all I'd admit to. Come to that, I could have given Granger the same reason now for manual landing instead of ditching. Everyone knew how mercenary I was. The trouble with that being that I wasn't sure Granger did know. He monitored most flights out of Home Base. He knew my standard line of patter about looking out for number one at any cost, but he also knew that I ended up with all the most hazardous runs. Whether they'd turn a profit or not. And particularly when the Company controller had assigned them to inexperienced pilots.

Moreover, Granger knew my nonexistent war record. Which was no secret: everybody knew my nonexistent war record. Hotshot Skyrider, the lady who couldn't make up her mind. Only I suspected Granger of having drawn some conclusion about that, beyond the obvious one that I encouraged. I didn't mind being thought a coward. I worried about what Granger thought instead.

My head hurt. I touched it absently, watching the flight deck, timing its spin. It was a huge flat-sided tunnel into the side of Home Base, one of the larger asteroids. The entire asteroid was honeycombed with tunnels; they formed the Company's central mining and transport offices and housed a lot of Company employees, including me. But the flight deck was the only tunnel open to space.

Of course, it wasn't really open; it was protected from the vacuum by a force screen that functioned like a semipermeable membrane, allowing shuttles through but containing the atmosphere within. Whenever a shuttle crossed the force screen, the people on the flight deck could hear an audible ''pop'' as the screen broke for it. A small amount of the interior atmosphere was lost each time, but not enough to inconvenience the ground crews.

My problem wasn't with the force screen; that would react automatically to alloys in the Ford's hull. My problem was that I had to exactly match the spin and velocity of the asteroid before I crossed the force screen. Like all the other asteroids in the Belt, Home Base rotated on an axis of its own while it revolved in its eccentric orbit around the sun. Some of them spin, some of them tumble, and some of them hardly seem to rotate at all. But most of the big ones rotate at a respectable speed. Home Base was no exception.

That was what the synch system was for. It synchronized the rotation of a shuttle with the rotation of an asteroid, and at the same time synchronized the revolution speed of the shuttle with the asteroid. "Catch and match." Catch up to it, in its solar orbit, and match its axial rotation before going in. I had a little leeway in the "catch" part. If I came in high enough, then even if I was going too slowly the force screen would give me the extra lift I needed to make the deck; and if I came in too fast, Flight Control could net me in the ground-based slowscreen. But there wasn't any leeway on the "match." If I was spinning too fast or too slowly when I hit the deck, I'd hit it like the proverbial shit hits the fan.

In fact, that's pretty close to what I was doing: trying to land a shuttle on one blade of a giant spinning fan. With a working synch system it was no big deal; it was all done by computers. Without a synch system, it was a quick ticket to hell. Most people had sense enough not to try it. We've already discussed how much sense I have.

The Comm Link was still open when I started my spin. I was close enough to the flight deck for visual scanning by then, and I heard Jamin curse when he saw what the Ford's belly looked like. "That's not just the synch system. She's lost half her controls. Flight Control, you'd better stop her. Nobody could land that thing."

I was too busy fighting my controls to answer him, but Granger said it for me: "The Skyrider can."

I hoped he was right. If he wasn't, I'd never know it. "Watch closely, rock jockey," I said. "This is what 'hotshot' looks like."

All of a sudden I could hear every damn Gypsy that ever roamed the Belt. They were singing for me.

A beautiful song, like the winds of space and the light of a million stars. Like the laughter in Django's eyes. Like living forever; and like dying for a dream.

I made one last adjustment, closed my eyes, drew my breath, and rammed the force screen. I think I was singing, too.

CHAPTER TWO

It wasn't exactly a textbook landing. My calculations were off somewhere by a very small margin. That's all it takes. We hit the deck portside-first and bounced in a shower of sparks. The whole shuttle groaned with the impact. I thought I felt the frame buckle. We slewed halfway around and skidded sideways along the landing panel in a howl of metal against metal that drowned the Gypsy chorus and all my inclination to sing.

The jockeystick slammed back against my leg. I cursed it and held on, using the thrusters to wrestle the Ford back over when she tried to roll. Something tugged at the starboard runner and we seemed to hang for a second, unbalanced, totally at mercy of whatever insane gods watch over shuttle pilots and fools. I had time to know we were going over. We had to go over. The thrusters had died without compensating enough for my error. Inertia will always win out in the end.

Then I felt the slowscreen lock onto us, just as the starboard runner came loose with a jerk that tilted us crazily to port. The gods were with me. That brief snag had straightened us on the panel, and the slowscreen was just enough of a balance to keep us from rolling. We were sliding head-on down the panel, miraculously right side up, miraculously whole. I didn't know whether the landing baffles would respond, but I hit the control just in case, and felt an answering tug as they snagged into the slowscreen currents. Then there was nothing left to do but watch the end-panel wall come at us, brace myself against my shock webbing, and curse. I'm very good at cursing.

We stopped exactly at the end of the panel, with the Ford's blunt nose pressed hard against the wall. It seemed very quiet out, all of a sudden. I released a breath I hadn't known I was holding and thought I heard an answering sigh over the Comm Link. "Welcome home, Skyrider," said Granger.

"Sorry if I scratched your panel." My voice wasn't quite steady. It hardly ever was when I was that surprised to be alive.

"That can be repaired," said Granger. "You'd better get clear; there's burn damage back here. You may have a fire down below."

"Thanks, guy." That meant he and the ground crews would cover for me. He couldn't say it any more clearly than that on the Comm Link. They would tell the Company that any burn damage to the Ford occurred on landing, not in space; which was a relief, because Jamin had been right when he said a wild rock couldn't have burned me. If I'd come in less spectacularly, I'd have had to find my own excuse. I'd been too busy to think about that, but Granger could hardly have covered for me if I'd made a standard synched landing; the Patrol was politically allied with the Company, and both agencies levied almost as severe a penalty for aiding a smuggler as for smuggling.

My head still hurt. And I had trouble unfastening my shock webbing; my hands weren't even as steady as my voice had been. Then I couldn't get the forward hatch open. The frame was buckled. I had to exit through the cargo hold. By the time I got out I really was ready to kill somebody.

Even in the normal course of events, with no smuggling side trips and no manual landings, I was often ready for a good fight after a long run. I usually found an excuse for it, but the plain fact was I tended to start swinging almost before I hit the deck. A lot of us did. I expect the real reason was just that a good fistfight helped ward off the moment when the adrenaline rush of risk-taking and lawbreaking wore off, and the inevitable post-run exhaustion set in. The exhaustion, and the shakes. I don't suppose I was the only pilot who got the shakes after a bad run, though it wasn't something we talked much about. Not even to each other. A rousing good fight seemed so much more gratifying. Well, nobody ever said we were mature. Anyway, nobody who knew us. It wasn't a line of work that attracted what the psych-tenders called a "stable element" of society.

Jamin was still on deck when I climbed down. He looked like as good a target as any. After our hurled imprecations over the Comm Link, maybe better than some. Besides, I didn't like the sardonic smile with which he greeted me. I stepped away from my battered Ford to let the ground crews at her and glared at Jamin. "I thought Granger said he was clearing out all nonessential personnel," I said. "You're about as nonessential as a personnel can get."

The Fire Control crew was liberally spraying the Ford with cooling foam, as if she were really on fire. Broken electrical connections sizzled and spat; ground crew members cursed, and somebody called my name from the ready-room door. I ignored that, blinking my light-dazzled eyes in an effort to keep glaring at Jamin. It wasn't easy, after hours in the cool dark of space, to look fierce in the blinding bright of the flight deck.

Jamin lifted his chin, maintaining the arrogant smile. His eyes were clear, shallow, unreadable blue. "Whatsamattayou, hotshot? You get somekine against me, or you just like make one big noise?"

I almost laughed at that. People who looked as aristocratic as he did usually spoke nothing but perfect Company English, as he had done on the Comm Link. "You talk Rock like a native," I said. "That's pretty quick work for somebody who just got hired. What've you done, two or three short runs so far? You know, it takes more than a couple of jumps and a smidgeon of pidgin to make you a Belter."

He dropped the Rock talk, and the smile. His eyes were still shallow, but there were shadows where there had been none. I was too angry to even guess at their meaning, and he wasn't telling. "What does it take?" he asked. "A few wrecked shuttles like that?" He gestured toward the broken Ford at my back. "Or would it be better if I lost a payload or two while I was at it?"

I swung without thinking. "I never lost a payload in my life, you bastard!" I lost Django, but that was different. And all the more reason for hitting.

Jamin didn't duck fast enough. I hadn't really hit very hard, but it nearly knocked him right over. At least it wiped the last trace of that mocking grin off his too-pretty face. I was about to follow through with a right hook that might have broken his jaw—and my hand—when somebody grabbed my arm from behind.

Somebody else caught my other arm, and a third somebody hooked a hand in my flight belt and jerked me away from Jamin. For a crazy moment I was fighting all three of them, trying to get at Jamin. Granger's little brother Bobby had stopped my right hook and still held my arm in a steel grip I couldn't break. He used his free hand to give me a good solid whack just over my ear. "Space it, Skyrider. Hang loose, okay?"

Jamin had finally recovered enough to try to take a swipe at me, but my good friend Magda held him back. His nose was bleeding. "Let me at her," he said, leaning against Magda's restraining arms in a convincing display of bravado now that the fight had been effectively forestalled. "I can take care of myself."

"Sure you can," Magda said soothingly. She jerked her head at Bobby and the others holding me. "Get the Skyrider out of here, guys. I'll take care of this one."

I didn't know what was going on, but I couldn't fight all of them, and after my first brief fury I wasn't fool enough to try. I settled for baiting Magda. "Whatsamattayou? 'Fraid I'll break your new toy?"

She frowned at me, shook her head almost absently, and had to concentrate on Jamin when my remark sent him into another fit of ineffectual rage. "Get her out of here," she said, shoving him bodily away from me. "Tell her, for the love of space."

"Tell me what?" I let them pull me away from Jamin. "What's going on? Why are you protecting that rock jockey?"

Bobby loosed his grip on my arm when he saw I was going obediently with them across the gleaming flight panels toward the ready room. "You can't fight Jamin on Company ground." He looked oddly embarrassed. "I'm sorry, Skyrider."

"Why the hell can't I? What's he to the Company? Some VIP's number one son?"

"Cousin," said Farley, the pilot who had held my flight belt and who now released it to walk beside Bobby.

"That, too," said Bobby. "But that's not why."

"So what is?" I shook my left arm free of Harrison, who lusted after my fair white body and didn't like to let go. "Why all the mystery? What's the big deal?"

"No big deal, exactly." Farley shook her long red hair out of her face and glanced back at Jamin, whose bloody nose was being ministered to by Magda and a deck med-tech. "It's just that Company ground is always kept at full Earth gravity."

"I know that. How else could the Earthers keep watch over all us dangerous Colonial-kine sympathizers?" They weren't about to trust the Belt to Belters, treaty or no treaty. The war had been fought, but none of the issues were resolved. Everybody had just got tired of dying. "We've been through all that before. What's it to do with Jamin?"

Bobby looked embarrassed again. Farley looked at the deck under her feet. It was Harrison who answered, his voice as unctuously earnest as always when he spoke to me. "He's a freefall mutant."

That got my attention. "He's what?" I couldn't believe I'd heard him correctly. A freefall mutant working out of a gravity station? "That's crazy."

Bobby shook his head. "Granger should've told you. He knew you'd come out fighting if you came out of that at all. And he could see Jamin would be handy."

We were at the ready-room door, and I had time to glance back at my poor ruined Ford before we went in. "Maybe he didn't think I'd make it."

"Nonsense," said Farley. "You always make it." She said it the way you'd say "space is a vacuum" or "Home Base is Company ground." Not anything to be particularly impressed with; just a fact of life. I liked that.

"You know that, and I know that." I grinned at her. "But there are always unbelievers."

"Granger isn't one," said Bobby, leading the way across the ready room toward my locker. "He must have forgot." He shook his head at his brother's negligence.

The ready room was one of the few Company areas designed for native Belters; which meant that its walls were unadorned rock and its furniture mostly polished metal. Even the cushions were friendly, familiar plastics, not the prickly furs and fabrics Earthers would choose. I took a deep breath, smelled the sweet damp tang of rock and metal, and relaxed a little. Maybe I hadn't really believed I'd make it home this time. But I was home, and I sat on the scarred metal bench in front of my locker without even trying to control my grin of relief.

Harrison, predictably, sat next to me. Farley and Bobby sat at the nearest gaming table and dialed soft drinks from the dispenser. I looked at them while I tugged off my flight boots. "Isn't anybody going to tell me why a rock-hopping freefall mutant is trying to work out of a gravity station? Surely he could find an easier way to suicide. Come to that, he could just space himself."

I thought, but didn't say, that if he'd been living under full Earth gravity for very long, he must want to space himself. The relief he would get in the freefall of short-running wouldn't be enough to live on. "Or have they invented more effective painkillers since my father's time?"

"More effective somekine, prob'ly," said Farley.

"But it still isn't easy. And it will kill him, soon or late."

"Then why does he do it?"

"His son is homozygous for gravity. A Grounder."

I stared at her, frowning. "That's impossible. A Faller can't have a Grounder kid."

She brushed back her hair. "Well, he's Jamin's stepson, really. Or his adopted son. I don't even know if he and the kid's mother were married. I just know she was killed in the war, and Jamin kept the kid."

"They were married," said Harrison. Longingly, I thought. He was watching me with his familiar lost-puppy expression, which always made me want to knock him down. No real reason. Grown men who could look like lost puppies just affected me that way.

I stood up to unzip my flight suit. It helped prevent unnecessary hitting by keeping my hands busy. "That's still no reason for a freefall mutant to live in Earth gravity. I mean, Grounders can live in freefall, if they have access to gravity and keep up their exercise. Otherwise the Belt would never have been colonized in the first place." All the early astronauts and colonists were homozygous for gravity. It wasn't until after the Belt was colonized that the freefall mutation had developed.

Since then, Humankind had been divided three ways: "Grounders" were gravity dwellers, most similar to the original Earther strain; "Fallers" were genetically adapted to freefall and could not tolerate gravity; and "Floaters" were a cross between the two. With one gene for gravity and one for freefall, we could "float" between the two environments at will.

I stepped out of my flight suit and pulled on a light tunic from my locker. "Jamin's the mutation, not the kid. Jamin's the one with limitations. Grounders are more limited than we are, since they have to have gravity sometimes, but for chrissake a Faller can't live in gravity at all!"

"He's doing it," said Bobby.

Farley made a face at him. "Watch the hero worship, kid. We have to live with death out here, but that doesn't mean we have to make a religion of it."

Bobby looked innocent. He was good at looking innocent. "What did I say?"

Farley shook her head. "Never mind." She looked at me and grinned ruefully. "In this crowd, nothing. I guess. But there is a difference between risking death and just plain buying it. I admire what you did out there, Skyrider. Prob'ly you're the only one of us who could have pulled that off. I hope you're the only one who'd try. And that's my point: what Jamin's doing . . ." She ran one hand through her hair, grimaced helplessly, and shook her head. "Oh, space. Creeping philosophy. I don't know what I'm talking about."

Harrison frowned earnestly. "He has to do it. The kid has some kind of inner-ear problem. He can't live in freefall, not even a little. Jamin's got to live in gravity, to stay with him."

"You think the kid'll be grateful when Jamin's dead?"

"What else is he supposed to do?" asked Bobby.

"I don't know," said Farley. "Don't get me wrong; I admire him for it. But I don't have to like it."

"Why, Farley, you surprise me." I belted my tunic and pulled on my slippers. "From what I saw of Jamin, I don't see how anyone could fail to like anything about him."

Farley grinned and threw her empty cup at me.

CHAPTER THREE

Home is a word people tend to use lightly. Home is where the hat is. Home is where one plans to sleep tonight. Home is where one stores one's tunics. It's just a word. It doesn't mean anything, really, to most people.

When I was Earthside, I found out it meant a lot to me. I was impressed with sky, enchanted with live ground covers, awed by mountains and miles and clouds and all the other alien wonders of Humankind's native habitat. But I wasn't at home. I was welcome, I was loved, I was accepted, and if not understood, I was anyway encouraged and supported. And I was out of place.

I just didn't belong on Earth. I belonged to the people well enough, and I was pleased and impressed with the land they lived on. I brought back a lot of holograms to remind myself how pretty it was. But it wasn't mine. It was fascinating, beautiful, friendly—and alien.

I could hear the Gypsies singing in my dreams at night the whole time I was Earthside. They sang of space. They sang of the safe boundaries of rock chambers and the prism colors of endless stars. They sang of the subliminal rumble of engines, the silent tumble and scurry of asteroids, the cold winds of a distant sun.

And they sang of Death. The Belters' forever enemy and companion. The dark face of freedom. The bargain a Belter has struck with the universe. Earthers died every day, same as anybody. But they didn't live on the raw edge of death the way we did.

All those Earth mornings I woke disoriented and lonely, and the love and acceptance of the Earthers around me wasn't enough to dissipate the loneliness. It wasn't just that I didn't know their rules: I could have learned those. Nor that I was nervous about all that open, unguarded, and unchambered air: I could have got used to that.

The plain fact was that I didn't really want to get used to it. I didn't belong there. I belonged in the Belt. In some indefinable way, the twenty years I'd spent out there had changed me. I wasn't an Earther anymore. I was related to Earth, and to Earthers, but I was not at home with them.

I didn't know, then, exactly what *home* meant to me, except that it didn't mean Earth. Now, relaxing in that rock-walled ready room, watching another cluster of pilots come in to settle at a gaming table with tall cold drinks from the dispenser, and credits from their last runs stacked up, ready to gamble away, I knew very well what it meant. I was born on Earth, but I came of age in rock-walled chambers like this one, with men and women like these for my companions and all the Belt for my playground.

That was *home*. And mirror-bright plasteel corridors that smelled of recycled oxygen and metal polish. A little half-furnished room where I hung my holograms. A shuttle in freefall. The unending thrum of engines and gravity generators; the unchanging temperature; the artificial, almost nonexistent difference between day and night. The knowledge that outside this rock wall, or that one, space was waiting. More than a place or a people, *home* meant a way of life. And Death for a neighbor. . . .

Which was all very fine and romantic, and it really only meant that I was, indeed, a hotshot pilot. I liked my life the way it was, and I didn't want to change it. And I was glad as glad to get back to it after my brief sojourn in the strange realm of Earth. In token of which I grinned at the new group of pilots and said, "Howzit?" in greeting, even though they included at least one with whom I'd done some really serious fighting in the past.

A couple of them glanced my way and nodded without interest.

"Cold caffeine?" asked Farley. I nodded, and she dialed it for me while I strapped on my handgun and closed my locker. I put my foot on the bench beside Harrison so I could strap down my holster, and wished I'd done it somewhere else when I saw that it was all he could do to keep his hands off me. He was a sorry specimen. Home Base was loaded with pretty pilots who'd have given their right gloves to go to bed with him, and he had to choose me, maybe the only one who didn't want him. Of course, that may have been why he wanted me. I gave him a meaningless grin and went to join Farley and Bobby at their gaming table.

It took Harrison a moment to decide whether to join us. He wasn't really as daft as he sometimes seemed. He knew damn well I didn't much care for him. The trouble was he cared for me—or rather for his image of me—enough to keep trying anyway. He decided to join us, with a fine show of confidence that he would be welcome and a pathetic old joke that fell flat.

Bobby broke the ensuing silence by asking me brightly, "How's Earth?"

"Hell of big," I said.

He made a face at me. "I meant—"

"I know," I said. "No politics, okay? Not here." Nobody had ever established whether the Company monitored our conversations in the ready room or in any other pilot territory. There was no real reason to think they would—and less to think they wouldn't. It would be easy enough, over the PA system. Any communications system could be made to work both ways.

"Yeah," said Harrison. "If they've had a look at that shuttle she brought in, they'll be hanging on her every word." He looked at me. "Where did they catch you, anyway? I'd have thought even in that old Ford, you could outrun the Pa—"

"Space it, jockey," said Farley.

Harrison's pretty brown eyes widened almost imperceptibly, and he blushed. Unbecomingly, I thought, though I knew a number of impressionable young pilots who would have disagreed with me. I wished he'd go find one of them. "Oh. Sorry," he said.

Whether or not there were Company officials listening, the pilots at the other table were. One of them said a little too loudly, "Yeah, Harrison. You know Melacha doesn't like to take sides."

"You trying to communicate anything in particular, Lunn, or d'you just like to hear yourself talk?" I looked at him over my caffeine glass, wondering whether he really wanted a fight.

Apparently, he wasn't quite sure himself. He blinked at me and said sullenly, "Everybody knows you've got Earther relatives."

"Has it escaped your attention that I live here?"

"Sure. And you think you're one big deal because you got enough pull with the Company, you don't even have to follow the Grounders' rules like the rest of us."

I put down my glass. "Which rules don't I follow?"

He shrugged, his little pig eyes blinking nervously. There was something very strange going on here. I'd had run-ins with Lunn before, and plenty of them, but they were spontaneous affairs like my altercation with Jamin. Lunn wasn't as stupid as he looked, but he wasn't bright, either, and he almost never resorted to words when action would do.

Yet he seemed to be trying to provoke an argument. And not just in words, which would have been odd enough, but in words that were very close to Company English. I hadn't known he could speak anything but the odd Belter argot we called pidgin. I'd never heard him speak English before.

Most Belters spoke some pidgin, but not all spoke English. Pidgin was the language of the Belt, a pastiche of the many languages that came out with the early settlers: Romani, Russian, Chinese, French, German, Portuguese, and just about every other Terran language, alive or dead.

Higher echelon Company employees were required to speak English, but pilots and miners and other manual-labor types didn't have to, if they could make themselves understood in their own language or in pidgin. Many of them spoke one or more of the other languages of Earth and learned Company English, if at all, as a second language. And there were a lot of Belters like Lunn whose native tongue was pidgin and who didn't bother with any other languages at all. At least, I hadn't thought he bothered.

"Which rules?" I asked again.

"Everybody knows you get first choice on shuttles."

"That's standard," said Farley. "She has the best flight record."

Lunn smiled, an unpleasant stretching of thick, tense lips. "Maybe. Before today."

"I got my cargo home." I was watching his eyes. They had an odd hooded look; almost intelligent. "Anyway, shuttle choice is pilot custom, not Company rule. Which Company rules d'you think I don't have to follow?"

If he'd been standing, I really think he would have shuffled his feet. "Well, um, you know, you don't even file one flight plan."

"I what?"

"And they don't check your shuttle for contraband."

"Who fed you this space dust?"

"And it's because they know you won't take sides. Hell, you didn't even fight in the war. But you won't be able to stay out of the next one."

"What next one? You have your own private war planned?"

He grinned again, exposing a tombstone row of yellowed teeth. "Maybe."

"He doesn't have to," said one of his companions.

I looked at her. She was another spaceborn Floater, usually less militant in her Colonial sympathies than Lunn was. "Why not, Annie? What's going on here? Did somebody start the revolution without me?"

"Somebody damn well will, if the Company doesn't ease up on freelancers," said Annie's current husband. I had forgot his name, but the thin white scar on his chin matched one on my knuckles. This was not my favorite crowd.

"They can't ease up on freelancers. They can't afford to."

"What business is it of theirs, anyway?" asked Lunn.

"They do run the Belt. They own most of the industry and a lot of the rocks. They're the government, for chrissake."

"A bunch of Grounders, what do they know how to govern the Belt? Half of the people out here have never been in gravity. Hell, half of 'em can't go in gravity. Why should people who aren't even able to visit Earth be governed by Earthers?" His name was Matt. I remembered now, because I'd made a pun about it the time I broke his jaw.

"They don't even speak our language," said Lunn. "We have to learn theirs."

"Pidgin isn't a language," I said.

"They don't own half the rocks," said Annie. "They took half the rocks. There's a difference."

"And they're trying to take the rest," said Lunn.

"By freezing out the freelancers," said Matt.

"But you know that, don't you, Skyrider?" said Lunn. My nickname never sounded like an insult before. "I mean, you're helping them. You don't give one damn if the freelancers starve."

"Wait a minute," said Farley.

"How the hell d'you think she got that Ford shot out from under her?" asked Bobby. "You think maybe she strayed into a military practice maneuver, or something?"

"Hey, space it, you guys," I said, conscious of the PA system over which some Company authority might be hanging on our every word. That might even explain why Lunn was making such an effort to speak English—though why he would join forces with the Company I didn't quite know. Anyway, nobody paid attention to my plea for silence.

"She only smuggles for the money," said Lunn. "She don't give one damn about the people."

"You're absolutely right about that," I said quickly. "If I were going to do anything as risky as smuggling, I can't think of a better reason than for the money."

"Yeah, but you don't do anykine risky, do you, Skyrider?" Lunn's ugly face took on an almost comical earnestness. "Like, for one thing, fighting in the war. You didn't do that. You couldn't choose one side back then, when it mattered. I lost many kine frien' in that war. What'd you lose?"

My self-respect, I thought, but I didn't say it. I was busy wondering why Lunn was so intent on goading me into a fight. And where the hell he got such intelligent verbal weaponry. "Me? I guess the biggest thing I lost was the war."

"You shoulda lost your Earth-loving life. You shoulda died." His expression went sly and secretive, but I wasn't ready for the next thrust anyway. "You shoulda died with that one Gypsy you killed, that's what you shoulda—"

Something snapped. I didn't hear the rest of what he said. I was kicking the tables aside to get at him. "You watch your mouth, rock slime, or you're the one who's going to die."

For a big man, he was surprisingly quick on his feet. Before I got to him, he was out of his chair, grinning that fat ugly grin, all decaying teeth and no brains. "Whatsamattayou?" he said, slipping back into pidgin now he'd got the action he was after. "I truth say, whatsamatta, you scare?" That's a literal translation; the actual words he used originated in three different languages, and the syntax in pidgin was even more confusing than I've represented it.

"You one truth say, rock slime. I that one Gypsy kill. And I now-time kill you, yes?" He was concentrating on my words, and he could really only concentrate on one thing at a time, even though I'd reverted to pidgin, too, to make it easy for him.

My slippered foot didn't do a lot of damage to his kneecap, but it helped distract him while I aimed a solid punch at his solar plexus and it connected with satisfying force.

The others were rapidly pulling the tables and chairs out of our way. Nobody made a move to interfere; that wasn't our way. They all knew I'd wanted a good fight since I landed. Fistfights were as natural and normal a part of our lifestyle as eating and drinking and flying. Another group of pilots had come in during our verbal interchange, too late to contribute materially to that. They made their contribution now by helping to get the furniture swept aside before either of us tripped on it.

That was standard procedure, but it seemed to irritate Lunn. He looked at them, completely forgetting me for a moment, his mean little eyes going beadier as his brows drew together in a bewildered, outraged frown. I didn't take advantage of his distraction, though I could have. I didn't just want to cream him; I wanted a fight.

When he remembered me, he ducked his head, scowled even more hideously, and came at me with a savage growl. He wasn't even looking where he was going. He meant to just bowl me over with sheer brute force.

I stepped aside. He didn't change direction. He

didn't even notice, I think. I put out one foot and braced myself. It was hardly my fault he tripped over my foot. If he'd had his eyes open, he could have avoided it. As it was, he went over headfirst and landed flat on his ugly face. He didn't even have time to put out his hands to break his fall.

This wasn't my idea of a reasonable way to conduct a fistfight, but what could I do? Lunn was never much good with his hands. I waited till he got back on his feet and lumbered at me again. And I hit him again. A left jab to the solar plexus, then a quick right hook to the jaw. This wasn't much fun. It was too damned easy. He didn't quite go down, but most of the fight went out of him.

It was always this way. He was a hulking great lummox, twice my size, and if he had got in one good solid punch, he could have had me on the floor in a minute. But instead of aiming any effective punches, he kept walking into mine.

"You want to quit while I'm ahead?" I'd waited till he had his feet back under him before I'd asked. Which was my mistake. I should have just hit him again and let it go at that. But no. Good old hotshot Skyrider always had to play fair, even with rock slime.

For my courtesy I got a force blade in the ribs. Oddly, it seemed he could move quite a bit faster with an illegal weapon in his hands. I could still move faster, but I hadn't been ready for a force blade.

I should have expected some kind of dirty trick. If I'd been a little more alert, he wouldn't have even nicked me. As it was, I jumped aside in time to save my life, but not in time to save all my precious bodily fluids. He maybe got one of my ribs, too; that wasn't clear. What was clear was that I was bleeding all over the ready-room floor, and I had a madman coming at me, intent on making me bleed a lot more. In other words, not a happy situation. I don't like bleeding. I really prefer to avoid it whenever possible.

It says something for the strength of our convictions and customs that I still didn't draw my handgun. I backed off with all prudent haste, but it just didn't occur to me to use a weapon. Not in the ready room; not in a fight with another pilot. Not even against a force blade.

The other pilots moved faster than I had. None of them drew weapons, either, but they moved. Life in the Belt often depended on an ability to grasp a new situation almost before it happened. They grasped this one before I did, and they tried to grasp Lunn. He wasn't having any. He damn near took off Farley's right hand with his blade, and he chopped off a corner of Bobby's tunic, just missing his leg. Then he was after me again.

I didn't make a very convincing effort to stop him. I was mostly intent on staying on my feet—and out of his reach. Neither thing was as easy as it should have been. Somebody reached for Lunn from behind, and he swung his blade around without looking. I couldn't quite see what happened, except that the other pilot fell away from him. There was a curious sparkling darkness before my eyes. I blinked, and Lunn was coming at me again. I had time to make a grab for his blade arm. He was damned good with that blade. He snicked it sideways, just a little twitch at just the right moment. Instead of grasping his blade arm, I almost grasped his blade.

Jerking away from that threw me off balance, but I aimed a solid kick at his kneecap anyway, wishing I still had my flight boots on. The blade had cut my wrist in that last maneuver. At this rate, even if he never got in a lethal jab with his little electronic wonder, I might bleed to death before I got him stopped. The kick at his knee missed altogether, and it damn near lost me my footing when I slipped in a splatter of my own blood on the floor.

The others were circling warily, making frequent attempts to rush Lunn, but he brandished his weapon with such indiscriminate viciousness that they couldn't even get close. Nor could I. Well, I'd asked for it. Hotshot pilot survives manual landing and dies in a ready-room brawl. What could be more fitting? I never expected to live forever, anyway. The only thing was, I'd really have liked to know why this was happening. Lunn and I had never been friends by any means, but he'd never shown homicidal tendencies before.

The question was academic. Maybe somebody else would find out afterward, but I'd never know. He was circling now, brushing off the other pilots, making his final approach for the kill, and I could barely see him through the spangled darkness that swirled before my eyes. I braced myself, determined to go down fighting, and blinked hard in an effort to clear away the stars. When I opened my eyes again, Lunn was gone. Just like that. One moment a mad lummox was bearing down on me with death in his eyes; the next, he was gone.

I blinked again, dizzily. There was a curious rushing sound in my ears, but otherwise the ready room seemed oddly silent. After a long, stupid moment I found Lunn. He was on the floor in front of me, out cold.

My heart hurt. I put a bloody hand on it and turned, swaying, to see what the hell was going on. The other pilots looked as surprised as I was, and nobody was stepping forward to take a bow. Everybody was staring at the doorway. It took me a moment to get sure enough of my balance that I could turn to stare at the doorway, too.

Jamin was there, with a stun gun still in his hand. Nobody spoke. I took my hand off my head. Jamin actually looked pleased with himself. I looked dizzily from him to Lunn and back again. "You stunned him?"

Jamin nodded, his smile gone a bit uncertain now that he noticed the general hostility he was facing.

"With that thing? You *shot* him?" I insisted.

Jamin nodded again, the smile gone completely.

I looked around at the others. A few of them were looking at me. Most of them were still staring in open shock and hostility at Jamin.

"You should have let me kill that son of a bitch when I landed," I said. "But it's not too late. Unless somebody still wants to protect the poor little freefall mutant?"

Most of them looked at me then. I noticed Magda on the far side of the room, looking with intent fascination at a bare patch of floor in front of her. Nobody came leaping to Jamin's defense this time.

CHAPTER FOUR

Most of us wore stun guns most of the time, strapped to our hips, like the Wild West cowboys of Earth legend. But wearing a gun and using a gun are two very different things.

Not that we didn't use them occasionally, when we had to. I used mine once, on a drug-crazed freelancer who couldn't pay for his supplies and didn't think to ask whether I'd extend him credit. And I knew Farley had used hers once, when a teen gang jumped her on Shangri-la with intent to do her grievous bodily harm, not to mention stealing anything of value she might be carrying. The Belt was still a frontier, not neat and orderly and safe and sterile like Earth or Mars.

But mostly our sidearms were a holdover from the war. One of the token concessions the treaty with

Earth had granted us was the right to bear arms, and we damn well bore them. That didn't mean we had to use them. And certainly not on each other. The taboo against that was so strong that I'd almost let Lunn kill me, without ever remembering I was wearing a weapon with which I could stop him. Maybe it should have occurred to me, but it didn't, and I'm not sure I would have used it if I'd thought of it.

Lunn had himself been using an illegal weapon, and I suppose I would have been justified in doing the same. Anyplace off Home Base, I probably would have done. But here I didn't think of it, and neither did any of the pilots in the ready room with me. One simply didn't. Not in the ready room, on Home Base, in a fight with another pilot. We were a rough-and-ready crew, but we weren't barbarians. Or cowards.

When I started toward him, Jamin raised his stun gun uncertainly. I stopped when he had it centered on my belly. He looked puzzled and angry, and not unwilling to use his weapon again.

"What the hell is going on here? Melacha?" he asked.

The barrel wavered, but not quite enough for me to take a chance on it. Particularly not since I was wavering too.

"Melacha, watsamattayou? What have I done now?"

I gestured at Lunn, a broad sweep of my arm that nearly toppled me. "That's what you did, rock jockey. Don't be stupid. You shot him."

Jamin's mouth quirked in half an arrogant grin. His eyes were shallow pools of deadly blue. The gun barrel wasn't wavering anymore. "He was going to kill you."

"That doesn't give you the right to shoot him."

"Well, you weren't doing it."

"Of course not," I said primly. "One doesn't, you know." I put a hand flat on top of my head. It didn't improve my balance. And the rushing sound in my ears was becoming a roar.

"Would you rather I let him kill you?"

Farley said unexpectedly, "He's new here. He's been living in the outer rocks. He really didn't know."

I couldn't see her. The red-starred darkness blinded me. "Outer rocks anykine cowards, then," I said . . . or tried to say. The gravity generator seemed to be malfunctioning. I couldn't tell whether I was floating or falling. And the peculiar roaring in my ears nearly drowned out all other sounds. Even my own voice. I reached for a chair to steady myself and misjudged the distance; the darkness confused me. "Bother." I realized I was falling, not floating. "Silly damn . . . bother."

When I could see again, there was a med-tech leaning over me. For some reason, mysterious to me at the time, I was stretched out as flat on the floor as poor Lunn, and about as helpless. My head hurt. As did my right side, my left wrist, and my right hand. I'd broken my knuckles on Lunn's jaw.

"Lie still," said the med-tech.

"Why should I?" I really didn't know.

"Because you've lost a lot of blood, broken at least one rib and one hand, and dented your thick skull on this chair before anyone could catch you.

I'm trying to paste you back together enough to get you to Sick Bay.''

"Don't need Sick Bay." But I waited till he finished taping my ribs before I sat up. "Where's that damned freefall coward?" I looked around dizzily. "And where's Lunn?"

"Lunn's gone to Sick Bay. You broke his jaw." Jamin loomed unexpectedly over me, displaying that infuriatingly sardonic grin. "And if by 'that freefall coward' you mean me, I'm right here." At least the gun was holstered.

"I can see that." I tried to look threatening, which was by no means easy when I was sitting on the floor getting pasted together by an attentive med-tech and Jamin was towering confidently over me. "Broke his jaw, did I?" I tried to push away the med-tech. He ignored my efforts. "Just wait till I get my hands on you," I told Jamin.

"Space it, Skyrider," said Bobby. "He didn't know any better. And he did save your life."

"Both irrelevant points," said Jamin. "I'll take you on any day, hotshot." He grinned wickedly. "But not before you've been to Sick Bay. I wouldn't want you to claim I had an unfair advantage. Besides, Cousin Willem wants to see you as soon as you're able. That's why I came down here in the first place. To tell you you're wanted at an emergency VIP meeting."

Cousin Willem. Cousin Board Member Willem. Farley had been right when she said Jamin had VIP relatives. Board Member is just about as VIP as a person can get, short of Board Chairman. Or President.

I pushed the med-tech aside and clambered to my feet, which maybe wasn't an altogether smart move; to keep from falling again, I had to grab the chair I'd banged my head on the first time.

"You okay?" asked Farley.

The med-tech was still fussing with my left wrist. I put my bandaged right hand on my bandaged ribs— many more bandages, and I'd begin to feel like a walking advertisement for spray-on sticking plaster— and managed to stand erect without support. I hurt, but I hoped that didn't show. "I'm just fine." I glowered at Jamin, defying him to contradict me. But my voice sounded thin and reedy. I cleared my throat and kept glowering. "If Willem wants to see me, why didn't he have me paged?"

"He did." Oddly, Jamin didn't look quite so superior as usual; he looked concerned. But he sounded superior. "You were so busy playing macho Skyrider with your fists, I guess you didn't hear him."

I took a swing at him, but dizziness made me clumsy. He caught my broken fist before it connected with his jaw, and held it, gently but inescapably. He was grinning again, mocking me. "Now I know you're okay." He sobered, still holding my hand. "Peace, Skyrider. Please?" There were unreadable shadows in the dark of those implacable blue eyes.

"Let go my hand." My voice was stronger now, even if I wasn't. The med-tech had given me a hypospray for the pain. It left me a little too happy, a little too uncertain of my limits.

Jamin watched my eyes for a long moment before he said again, "Peace?"

The mockery was still there, but with shadows in it. My gaze faltered. I couldn't convincingly glower at a man with eyes like that. Reluctantly, I nodded. "Peace." I looked away. "For now."

He let go my hand. Cautiously. And I, equally cautiously, withdrew it from his reach. But I didn't look at those eyes again.

"Willem really does want to see you," he said. "But maybe you should go to Sick Bay first."

"You certainly should," said the med-tech.

"Later." I managed a sardonic grin of my own. At least, I hoped it was sardonic. "One can't keep a Company VIP waiting."

"The Skyrider can." The tone of his voice startled me into looking at him, but his expression was only mildly amused.

"Space yourself, rock jockey." Still, I blushed at the compliment. Beside me, Farley was grinning. I looked around. They were all grinning. "Space all of you," I said sullenly. Which only made their grins widen. "Bother." I glanced at Jamin. "Lead on, Company kin." He led. I followed, manfully containing my enthusiasm. A call to visit Willem in person could only mean trouble, and I'd had quite enough of that for one day.

Probably Granger's story about the burn damage to the Ford hadn't held up. It was a pretty open secret that I did my share of smuggling; most of the good pilots did. The main thing was never to get caught with the evidence. The Company could suspect all it wanted, but as long as nobody could prove anything, we were okay. If somebody had managed to prove it

was a Patrol blast rather than my landing that burned
the Ford . . .

"Why so serious?" asked Jamin.

I glanced at him, then quickly away again. Those
eyes were too startlingly blue, too aloof, too vulnerable.
I couldn't look at them. "No matter."

"That pilot hurt you."

"I'll live."

"If I was really out of line to shoot him, I'm
sorry."

I shrugged, and immediately regretted the gesture;
it hurt. "You saved my life."

"A little while ago you were ready to kill me for
it."

I grinned. "I can change my mind, can't I?"

"I guess you can."

We walked in silence after that, and I had time to
wonder again what could be proved from that burn
damage to the Ford. And to notice that despite whatever new medication had been invented for freefall
mutants since my father's time, Jamin walked with
the same awful delicacy my father always had. His
movements were lithe and graceful, but with an
underlying caution: he was an alien in this place, not
walking on thin glass, but rather made of it. In
freefall he might be as tough as anybody, certainly as
tough as I. But under the strain of Earth gravity he
was fragile, horribly breakable. And always in pain.

"It isn't about your shuttle," he said suddenly.

"What?" That caught me completely by surprise.

"The meeting. I don't know what it's about, but I
know it isn't about your shuttle. They might suspect,

but they can't prove anything. The ground crews covered for you. And apparently nobody was listening when I opened my big mouth on the Comm Link."

"How d'you know? Did you ask Cousin Willem?"

He looked at me. I could feel him looking at me, but I refused to meet that blue gaze. "No." His voice was cold, hard, distant. "No, I didn't ask Willem."

"Well, thank God for small favors."

"You know," he said conversationally, "you are probably the most arrogant, self-centered, unpleasant woman I have ever had the misfortune to meet."

I grinned at that. "Yeah. I'm real fond of you, too, rock jockey. Real fond."

I don't know what he would have done with that if we hadn't arrived just then at the door to the VIP meeting room. Since we had, he had time only to frown at me before I opened the door for him with a flourish—and a groan, because the hypospray for pain wasn't all *that* good—and we went in.

The VIP meeting room was an Earther area, radically different from pilots' territory. It might have been a room in an office building on Earth, for all the rock left showing. There wasn't any, not even the floor, which was tiled with gleaming squares of rich burnished brown tones meant, perhaps, to simulate wood. The walls were paneled with what looked like genuine wood, in muted shades of gold and tan, and hung at intervals with framed works of art in the popular nouveau-surrealist style. One repellant hodge-podge of stars, eyes, hair, and gaping mouths briefly caught my attention with its unsettling colors of blood and shadow.

But the real crowning glory of those walls, discomfitting to a Belter and doubtless very soothing to the Earthers, completely destroyed all possibility that the smaller works might receive more than a brief glance of appreciation or disapprobation.

The whole far wall was made to look like a window. And not a window into space, which I'd have found pleasant enough, if a bit odd here, so far from the outer walls of Home Base. This was a window onto Earth.

A view from a distance might have been nice: Earth is a lovely planet, with its great whorls of white cloud cover shrouding the gentle blues and greens of its beautiful seas. But this "window" looked out as if, I suppose, from an actual office building, perhaps to complete and enhance the general impression given by the overall decoration of the room. Perhaps it comforted and reassured homesick Earthers to imagine they were on the top story of one of NYork's towering plasteel structures, looking out over the city and the sky.

White and gray dollops of cloud floated aimlessly in a brown-tinged blue atmosphere; spires of plasteel thrust their reflective walls up at the sky like blunt, broad battering rams meant to plunge the clouds up into the stratosphere. And below, so far below they looked like children's plastic toys, the endless stream of electric autos and bright-garbed pedestrians swarmed through the narrow shadowed streets on their earnest, aimless errands.

That caught me up short. I could not, while gazing into that too-effective hologram, force my feet to carry me farther into the room. It bothered Jamin, too; apparently, though, he'd seen it before, because he didn't let himself be trapped by vertigo. After one involuntary glance he averted his gaze and unobtrusively grasped my elbow, an unexpected but most welcome gesture of support and reassurance.

With a supreme effort I dragged my gaze from that horrific display, back into the quiet chamber with its genuine mahogany conference table and plush gold metal and velvet chairs. Willem wasn't waiting for us alone in there. A whole gaggle of VIPs were seated around the table, with pads of real paper and mechanical pencils in front of them just as if they all had something important that they might need to write down at any moment. There was a big pitcher of ice water in the center of the table with ordinary drinking glasses grouped decoratively around it in case anybody got thirsty. I could only guess that a computer terminal for each of them, in place of the pads and pencils, or a dispenser in place of the pitcher and glasses wouldn't have had enough class for such an august company.

"Sorry we took so long, Willie," said Jamin.

Willie. Jamin showed some promise after all. I grinned.

Willem gave Jamin a look replete with censure and disappointment. "I have asked you repeatedly," he began, and let his voice trail off as he noticed me. "My God."

"No, I'm just the Skyrider; God was busy, so She

sent me." I grinned at him. "What can I do for you?"

"She'd look better if she'd let Sick Bay take care of those injuries," said Jamin. "But she wouldn't go."

"Why not?" That was Willem's wife Agatha, whose plump black wrinkled face looked very like an animated prune, with a startling fringe of soft white hair to emphasize its sharp sagging lines. I'd always wondered why she couldn't have something done about that. She was a fine one to ask about avoidance of med-techs. A simple face lift might have made her look human. She had beautiful skin; if only she hadn't quite so much of it.

I shrugged. "I didn't want to keep such an important group waiting. What's on?"

Agatha pursed her lips and looked away, perhaps as a sign of distaste for my casual language. Willem was still goggling at my bandages. The others at the table were, in order from Agatha around to Willem beside her: Kethen Dreed, a high muckymuck in the Patrol; Pete Francis, a former freelancer who'd struck it rich and bought into the Company at a very high level; Uluniu, whose specialty was politics and who called herself an ambassador-at-large; and a rotund woman with pink cheeks and shrewd eyes, whom I'd never seen before.

Uluniu saw the direction of my gaze and said hastily, "Susan Kokua, Melacha Rendell. Susan is with Interplanetary, Incorporated." She sounded as though that should make clear to me the reason for Kokua's presence at a Company VIP meeting, but it didn't make anything clear to me at all. I didn't see why any of them should be there, except Willem and maybe Agatha. What did the rest of them care if I'd crashed a shuttle?

"I assume you've seen the newsfax," said Kokua.

I looked at her. "Not lately. I've been on a run."

She looked surprised and transferred her gaze to Jamin. He shook his head, smiling just as arrogantly at her as he had done at me. "I've been on a run, too."

"I assume you refer to some form of acceptable behavior?"

"They mean they've been flying, yes," said Uluniu. "It's how pilots refer to a ru—er, that is, to a particular flight."

"I see." Kokua looked at me again. Those eyes were deadly. She might be rotund, and her cheeks might be baby pink, but I sure wouldn't have wanted to meet her alone in a dark corridor anywhere. "Then you don't know about the *Marabou*?"

"I know it's a liner. Runs between Earth and Mars, right?"

She frowned. "It does." She looked surprised. "It did. . . . That is, yes, the ordinary route of the *Marabou* is between Earth and Mars." But she still looked surprised, and maybe irritated.

"Its ordinary route?" asked Jamin. "What's that mean?"

But Kokua was still worrying about what she'd already said. After a silent moment, during which Uluniu suddenly remembered to offer Jamin and me chairs—and we accepted them—Kethen Dreed answered Jamin's question for Kokua. "It means the *Marabou* is in trouble. We don't know whether she can be saved. She was on a routine run to Earth." She glanced at Kokua when she said "run"; but Kokua was still lost in her own thoughts, oblivious to the rest of us. "We think she was sabotaged. Anyway, the engines are badly damaged, and both pilots were killed. It's not clear what exactly happened. The crew is working on the engines now, but they don't have all the materials they will need to repair them. Even if they had, and could complete the repairs, there is no one left on board the *Marabou* who knows how to pilot her." She didn't have to complete that thought. Without a pilot, the *Marabou* would miss Earth orbit and continue to fall insystem, eventually into the sun.

Nobody said anything for a while. I thought of a lot of things it wouldn't have been prudent to say. Jamin looked arrogant and disinterested. The VIPs looked uncomfortable.

"There are three hundred civilian passengers on board the *Marabou*," Pete Francis said, breaking a silence that was becoming decidedly awkward.

"And the payload," began Agatha.

"Passengers are payload," Pete said quickly.

That was interesting. I looked at Agatha. "The payload?"

She looked at Pete.

"You might as well know," said Dreed. "You'll learn eventually. The remaining payload is of crucial military and scientific importance to both Earth and the Company."

I nodded. "In other words, something Colonial Insurrectionists would be glad to see lost."

"But the passengers," said Pete.

"It does explain the sabotage," said Jamin.

"If it was sabotage," said Pete.

"I can't believe that even the Insurrectionists would risk the lives of three hundred civilians, just to stop that payload," said Uluniu.

I looked at Jamin. An Earther payload explains the sabotage, does it? I wished I knew which side he was on. A Faller with a Company VIP in the family could go either way. "Depends on the payload," I told Uluniu. "It must be something pretty damned important."

"It is," said Willem.

"But so many civilians," said Uluniu.

"How many civilians died when the Company cut off the freelancers from all legal sources of supply?" I asked.

"They were given ample opportunity to come in," said Agatha.

"Opportunity to give up everything they'd worked for all their lives," said Jamin. "Their mines, their homes, their businesses, their freedom—"

That might indicate which side he was on. Or it might just be a lot of words. One really couldn't tell from his expression. Arrogant, as always. But he hadn't told them I was a smuggler. Of course, he didn't have to tell them; if they didn't know, they were fools.

"How many civilians died when the Patrol blasted Shanghai II out of the Belt?" I asked. These were all old issues, but we weren't trying to solve anything here. We were just sizing each other up.

"There was adequate reason to believe Shanghai II was a military stronghold of the Insurrectionists," said Dreed.

"How many civilians die every day, right now, in military prisons and detention camps and forced-labor crews, because they broke some obscure, irrelevant, impossible Earther law?"

"Skyrider," said Jamin.

I looked at him. "How many freefall mutants—"

"Skyrider."

I shrugged impatiently and shut up. It was Willem who finally broke that silence. "Do you want those three hundred civilians to die, Melacha?" The use of my name was a gentle reprimand.

"What the hell can I do about it?"

"You could go after them," said Uluniu.

I stared. First at her, then at Dreed. "That's the Patrol's job, surely?"

Dreed looked embarrassed and neglected to respond. Kokua had finally regained her voice, though. "The military had its chance." Her voice was bitter, those sharp little eyes deadly. "They sent out two persons who they claimed were their best pilots, in a Falcon, which is said to be their best ship. The mission was a failure."

"What happened?"

Dreed looked defensive. "They *were* our best pilots. But without a pilot on board the *Marabou*, the synch system is worthless. Our pilots tried a dead-docking, and both were killed in the attempt."

"So you want me to try it." I looked at Willem. "You decided I could do it. Why? Because I managed that manual landing today? Or is it just that I'm expendable? What the hell, you lose a potential Colonial sympathizer, what's the big deal, right?"

"Skyrider," said Jamin.

"That's my name." I was losing patience with him. "Don't wear it out."

"But—"

"You heard them. They want me to dead-dock with a damn liner in flight, to save their precious payload."

"To save the civilians," said Pete.

"You've already lost two military pilots, and whether they were the best or not, I don't imagine they were rookies. Two experienced test and rescue pilots, right? They failed, and you want me to do what they couldn't do? What no sane pilot would even try to do?"

"No further military efforts will be made," said Dreed.

"The payload is of greater importance to the Company than to the military," said Agatha, prune-faced.

"And to whom are all those passengers important?" I asked.

"To you, we'd hoped," said Pete.

"Melacha, we know what your sympathies are, but, that is," said Uluniu, and wavered into awkward silence.

"And if I did try it? I don't know how to pilot a damn monster liner."

"I do," said Jamin.

I looked at him. "Sweet Jesus."

"That, too," Pete said seriously.

"But how do we know the military effort didn't damage the *Marabou*'s docking facilities?" asked Jamin.

"We don't," said Willem.

Jamin shifted uneasily on his chair. "Even if there's no damage, I don't quite see how you think anybody could dead-dock with a liner in flight. I doubt if there's a pilot in the Belt foolish enough to try. And if there is, he's crazy. Nobody could do it."

Willem looked at me. "The Skyrider can."

I made a rude noise. I'd heard that line once too many times today. I'm as susceptible to flattery as the next guy, but there is a limit. "Wait a minute, here, folks. I am one damn good pilot, sure. But I don't volunteer for suicide missions. I don't know whether Jamin's little speech was intended as a dare or just as an insult, but it doesn't matter. Either way, I'm not taking the job. I may be the best there is, but I ain't that good. Or that stupid. And I'm real fond of living. So just find yourself some other sucker, okay? I don't give a damn whether your precious payload makes it to Earth or not." I glanced at Pete. "And as for your passengers, they're just out of luck. Accidents happen. They knew that when they boarded. If they've been dealt a bad hand, that's not my problem. I'm nobody's nanny. And I'm no test and rescue pilot, not by a long shot. I'm not going."

"Skyrider!" Jamin's tone was considerably altered by my outburst.

"You finished?" asked Pete. He was trying not to grin.

"I'm not going. That's final. Jamin says he can pilot the liner. Fine. Let him dock with it, too."

"Now are you finished?" asked Pete.

"I'm leaving." I didn't move.

"How much?" asked Agatha. She looked like she'd swallowed a hot rock.

"How much what?" asked Dreed in surprise.

Jamin stared. "You're kidding!"

I just looked at them.

"Two months' wages," suggested Willem.

I went on looking.

"At risk rates," said Pete.

When nothing further seemed forthcoming, I said grimly, "Risk is right. And I ain't taking it."

"What, then?" asked Willem.

"You're serious," said Jamin.

"Are *you* going to do it?" I asked him.

"I doubt if I could dock with a liner," he said in surprise. "I'd like to go along, though. To pilot her. Three hundred civilians . . ."

I looked at Willem. "I want a Falcon."

"Done," he said.

"Not just for the mission. I want all its papers. In my name. Permanently."

He swallowed. Pete looked at him, and he looked at Pete.

"Are you actually bargaining with this upstart?" asked Dreed.

I smiled at her. "It's that or do without me. This isn't the military. I can't be ordered to kill myself.

They have to ask. And if I feel like living, all they can do is bargain or fire me." Still grinning, I looked at Willem. "They aren't going to fire me. That they really can't afford."

"In your name, permanently," said Willem. "Yes, all right, but that's it. No more."

"More. I want the Company's guarantee to maintain and repair my Falcon exactly as it would a Company shuttle. For as long as I remain employed by the Company."

"That's too much," said Agatha.

I stood up. "Find somebody else."

I was halfway to the door before Willem said, "Only if you use it on Company business."

I turned around. "Even if I use it for pleasure."

He hesitated. I started to turn again. "You will use it for your regular runs?" he asked plaintively.

"Sure. But if it gets damaged on a pleasure jaunt, I want the Company to repair it. And I want regular maintenance, in any event."

He looked at Pete again, and Pete looked at me. "It's ready and waiting," he said, "down on Alpha Seven. I'll have it flown up to Home Base by morning." He wasn't trying to conceal his grin anymore. There was no reason to conceal mine.

CHAPTER FIVE

"I don't believe you did that." Jamin was incredulous and angry, which was actually something of an improvement over arrogant and aloof.

We were on our way to pilot territory, walking together only because we'd left the VIP meeting at the same time and were both going in the same direction. It would have been awkward to try not to walk together. But he was doing his best, whenever we met anyone in the corridors, to look like he didn't know I was there and wouldn't recognize me if he did.

"You don't believe I did what?" I knew perfectly well what was bothering him, but I felt like making him say it.

"You bargained with them!"

I've heard people speak of murder with less distaste.

"Three hundred people's lives are at stake, and you bargained for a shuttle before you'd go after them!"

"That's what I did. And you volunteered to give your sweet all, to go on what amounts to a suicide mission, for nothing more than standard hazardous duty pay. The Company would have given you twice that, or more, if you'd asked."

"So now it's a suicide mission." He smiled grimly. "From all I've been told about the Skyrider"—he made that sound like a curse—"I assumed there was little or no risk involved. Surely a dead-docking procedure, even with a liner in flight, will be child's play for someone of your talents."

I looked at him, trying to read those incredible eyes. "I said before it was a suicide mission. I meant it. The docking will be no real problem unless those military idiots fouled the equipment in their attempt. But stop and think about it. Once I've docked, we'll be there. On the *Marabou*. Falling insystem. What if the engineers can't mend their precious engines in time?"

He hesitated. "If you can dock, you can release, can't you?"

"Why bother? Sure, maybe I could. Maybe I even would. But we're talking about your life, not mine."

He frowned at me, those eyes bewildering in their intensity. "So what difference does that make?"

"Don't be stupid." Oddly, in spite of the antagonism between us, I didn't like to put it into words.

"I'm not being stupid. Ignorant, maybe. What in space are you getting at?"

He just hadn't thought it through. He'd got so intent on those three hundred civilians Pete kept harping on, he'd forgot his own limitations. I thought about it, trying to find a way around the obvious. There was none. "There's a little matter of fuel," I said at last.

"In a Falcon? You're kidding. We'll have plenty of fuel to get there. And to get away again, if we have to."

"To get away where, Jamin?" I didn't look at him while he thought about it. I couldn't. From as far insystem as we would be when we caught up with *Marabou*, the only place we'd be able to reach would be Earth. And Jamin was a freefall mutant.

"Oh." We walked in silence for a while after he'd figured it out. "Well, we could refuel at a space station and make it back to the Belt." He wasn't thinking clearly at all.

"In a Falcon?" Falcons didn't dock with space stations. Another inconvenient holdover from the Incident, when all the Falcons were in Insurrectionist hands.

"Well, with a liner, then. Through a liner to a space station."

"If we happened to find a handy liner that had time to accomodate us, that might work."

He shrugged that away. "Even if we didn't, even if we had to go to Earth . . . well, it wouldn't kill me. This is Earth gravity here."

"It wouldn't kill you. Not for a while. But . . . forever?" I was thinking about my father. He was a Faller who went to Earth under just such circumstances as we were discussing. It was one thing for a freefall mutant to visit, or even to live on, a rock that was kept at full Earth gravity. If things got too rough, he could always turn off the gravity generator. Or if he hadn't individual controls for that, he could take a shuttle ride in freefall. Not all gravity stations had freefall sections, but in a shuttle you could always turn off the generators. Not only were there a lot of pilots who were Fallers, but there were also a lot of payloads that required freefall. A rock could have a generator with no switch, but a shuttle couldn't.

On Earth, the planet itself was the gravity generator. Nobody could turn that off. And no freefall mutant had ever survived the stress of the multiple gravity forces exerted upon anyone leaving Earth. The ship hadn't yet been built that could climb up out of that gravity well without crushing a Faller. And my father's dream of a reverse generator powerful enough to protect Fallers was still just that: a physicist's dream.

Jamin actually managed to grin. "Well, at least I'll have a choice, won't I."

"Sure. Fry or be squashed."

"You certainly do have a way with words."

Before either of us could say anything more, a towheaded whirlwind arrived and nearly bowled Jamin over with the force of a delighted greeting hug. "Papa! Where have you been, I thought you were supposed to be back hours ago, I have pictures to show you, I thought you'd never get back, where have you *been?*" I'm sure the boy never saw the fleeting look of agony that twisted Jamin's face when that whirlwind hug hit him. But I saw it. He hadn't been ready for that.

He recovered quickly, though, and in one graceful, smooth motion picked the boy up, whirled him around, and put him back down again in front of us. And I wasn't ready for the look on Jamin's face when he introduced his adoptive son to me. Those tormented eyes had lost their shadows. The man was actually smiling. A pure, radiant smile of delight that utterly transformed his features.

"Melacha, I'd like you to meet my son Collis." They stood together, with Jamin's hand on Collis's shoulder and Collis's arm stretched up to reach around Jamin's waist. *These two against the universe* . . . "Melacha," Jamin told Collis, "is one of the other pilots here at Home Base."

Collis looked at me. His eyes were as implacably blue as Jamin's, but that and the look of love were the only ways in which they looked alike. Collis was a little blond, baby-faced sweetheart, totally unlike his gaunt, dark-haired adoptive father. He won me over, heart and soul, with just one blinding smile, which was also quite a difference from the way Jamin had affected me on first meeting.

As I looked at the two of them together I realized I was maybe going to have to reassess my evaluation of Jamin. I'd thought of him as an arrogant ex-military jock with no redeeming qualities whatsoever, unless one counted his willingness to risk his life for those passengers on the *Marabou*. That might or might not have been a redeeming quality, depending mostly on his motives, which I hadn't come near to figuring out.

But standing here, arm in arm with that trusting little boy, he didn't look like an arrogant jock anymore. And it occurred to me, as it might have done hours ago if he'd for one minute been pleasant to me, that the cold look of aloof detachment Jamin habitually displayed might after all be a result of pain, not arrogance. It might be only a freefall mutant's self-conscious attempt to appear at ease in gravity. Pride will do that. We all knew he was an uncomfortable alien in this environment. But pride might make him prefer to be disliked for arrogance rather than pitied for suffering.

Collis interrupted my wandering thoughts with a delighted cry of recognition. It hadn't escaped my attention that Jamin carefully introduced me by name. But evidently Collis had heard of me elsewhere. "Melacha Rendell?" he asked. "Gosh, you mean the Skyrider?" He transferred his gaze from Jamin to me. "Is that who you are? The Skyrider? The pilot who brought in the *Sunjammer*? And rescued that lifeboat from the *Big Eagle*? And—"

"Hold it, hold it." I laughed, enchanted by those remarkable blue eyes, so very like Jamin's and yet so different. "Yes, I'm the Skyrider. And I helped bring in the *Sunjammer* and a lifeboat from the *Big Eagle*. A couple of other infamous exploits usually get credited to me along with those. But I had a little help on all of them, you know. And I hope my mistakes never get as famous as my achievements."

"Papa says you're prob'ly the best pilot in the

whole Belt." That startled me into staring at Jamin, who avoided my gaze while Collis went on, "But I think he is. I mean, everybody knows you're good, but did you know Papa brought down three Earth Fighters in just one battle during the war?"

"Collis," Jamin said in a quelling tone.

"Three? In one battle?" I said.

Collis nodded, smug with pride. "And one time when my mom and Papa were running guns to Mars—"

"Collis," said Jamin.

I grinned at the boy. "I think he's getting modest."

Jamin turned, still resting his hand on Collis's shoulder, and started on down the corridor in the direction we'd been going. "Mostly I'm getting hungry," he said, still not looking at me. "Have you eaten, Collis?"

Collis reached out a hand to me as I fell in step with them. "Not lately." He smiled up at me. "That's his standard excuse. But really, Mom and he were running guns and the EFs caught up with them—"

Jamin interrupted, blushing furiously. "I doubt if the Skyrider's interested in that, Collis."

"Oh, but I am."

"I know," said Collis. "What they did, Mom and he were in stolen Starbirds and they led the EFs right into a bunch of wild rocks to confuse their instruments, you know, and then Papa dodged them while Mom dropped behind and blasted them right out of the Belt." He sobered briefly. "That was before Mom died." Those wide blue eyes turned trustingly toward me. "The EFs got her. On another run. And Papa caught up with them and blasted every last one of them, and then he tracked down a bunch more of them and he just kept fighting till he didn't have any more fuel or anything, because he was saving a whole platoon of Colonists that were trying to hold a rock over by New England, and then they had to save him and they found out the Earthers had shot holes in his engines and a piece of flak went right through his leg and all he did about it was sealant the cockpit before all the air got out and then kept fighting.''

Jamin tried again. "Collis . . ."

I laughed. "It's okay; you're saved. For now. This is my door, and I'm hungry, too." I squeezed Collis's hand before I let it go. "But I want to hear more about your father's exploits," I told him. "We could sneak out for a soda sometime when he's working; that way he wouldn't keep trying to interrupt you."

"You've heard all there is." Jamin was trying to look arrogant again, but it didn't work, and he knew it. He gave it up and grinned at me. "To hear Collis tell it, I'm one of the all-time heroes of the war."

"Well, it's true," said Collis.

"I believe you." I meant it. I was beginning to realize how very severely I had misjudged Jamin. Obviously, there was a lot more to him than those blue eyes would ever willingly reveal. I smiled at them both and turned toward my door, but Jamin stopped me.

"Skyrider."

Startled, I turned back to look at him. "Yeah?"

"Go to Sick Bay, damn it. Get those broken bones healed, at least. You've proved your point, you know."

90

I'd have punched anybody else for saying that. I might have punched him, if Collis hadn't been there. And he knew it. Those eyes weren't so inscrutable after all. They were laughing at me. But not mocking, not anymore.

Reluctantly, I nodded. "Yeah, okay. After dinner."

He looked at me for a long moment, judging my expression, before he nodded and turned away.

As I was opening my door I heard Collis ask him how long he was going to be home this time. I paused in the doorway long enough to hear his answer. "I'm sorry, son. Not long, I'm afraid. The Skyrider and I have a mission that can't wait."

The look on Collis's upturned face brought unexpected tears to my eyes. It had been a long time since I'd seen love like that. Too long. Playing cowboy was a lonely damn way to live.

And if it was hard on me, a grown woman who made her own choices and lived with them, what must it be for Collis? He didn't choose this life. He had no control over it. And the awful disappointment, quickly and bravely concealed but not quite quickly enough, told what it cost him. Poor kid, he didn't choose any of this.

I could see Jamin's face only in profile, but that was enough. He'd seen the boy's disappointment, and it hurt him. At that moment they looked terribly alike in their attempt to protect each other with false good cheer. I closed my door and leaned against it, put a hand flat on top of my head, and angrily blinked away tears. What the hell was I crying for?

Because I wasn't loved like that? I didn't want to

be loved like that. I knew what love was like. I'd been there. (The image of Django's smile dazzled me for a moment, until I opened my eyes.) Love like that could drag one down. It had nearly dragged me down. I didn't want that again. If Django were still alive, sure, I'd be in his arms in a flash. But he wasn't, and I wasn't. I was alone, and by God I liked it that way.

Somebody once said loners are losers. Maybe that was right; maybe we were. But I didn't feel like a loser. I had just run the biggest bluff I'd ever pulled on the Company, and I'd won. In exchange for a job they should have known I'd do anyway, I would be given my own private Falcon, with guaranteed Company maintenance. Who could ask for more?

The job itself wouldn't be easy, but nobody asked for easy. I was pretty sure I could do it, and I knew I'd have fun trying. An odd way to think of it, maybe, to say I'd have fun risking my life on a mission at which trained test and rescue pilots had already failed. But that was how I felt about it.

Oh, I was scared, too. I don't deny that. Maybe that was even part of the pleasure of it. And I was introspective enough to wonder just what sort of person this Skyrider was, this woman who never felt so much alive as when she was in immediate danger of dying. If there was an answer, I didn't find it. That was how I was, and maybe there wasn't an answer to why.

The VIPs should have remembered that. They should have known I'd go after the *Marabou*, Falcon or no Falcon. I'd never admit it now, of course. But I was well enough known for taking chances nobody else would take, for gambling with destruction just so I could revel in the thrill of cheating Death. They should have remembered.

When I told the VIPs I didn't volunteer for suicide missions, I told the truth. Maybe they forgot that one way or another I always seemed to end up on suicide missions anyway. Which was exactly what the *Marabou* mission was. If they wanted to give me a Falcon for it if I survived, why should I argue?

If I survived, I'd have earned it.

CHAPTER SIX

After dinner I went to Sick Bay, where they mended my broken bones and completed the patch job the med-tech had started on my various other cuts and bruises. I came away pasted much more convincingly (and much less showily) together, with a last painkilling hypospray keeping me happy and a mild sedative to promote a good night's sleep.

Since the sedative was administered by the psych-tenders rather than the regular med-techs, I felt safe in assuming its main purpose was really to keep me from dwelling on things, past and future, over which I had no control. That was as well; I did have a tendency to dwell. The psych-tenders had long been assuring me that that regrettable proclivity was the primary cause of my recurring headaches. I often came away feeling like a recalcitrant child. They were so comically stern in their little lectures. I must learn to relax, they told me severely. I must learn to release and express my emotions. I must eat well, sleep well, worry (if I must worry at all) only about those things over which I had some degree of control. And most of all, I must relax!

There's something very contradictory in being ordered to relax. But that night, perhaps because of the sedative, I had every intention of following their instructions to the letter. I didn't have a headache, or any other aches. I did have a new puzzle to solve, because when I inquired after Lunn I learned that he'd recovered and fled Home Base in a stolen shuttle—which was not like Lunn at all—but I didn't feel like worrying that one tonight. All I really wanted to do was to go home and get about eighteen hours' sleep.

I'd managed perhaps eighteen minutes' sleep, at best, when the door chime woke me. Despite the various medicinal chemicals polluting my bloodstream, I woke instantly and completely. Even a second's disorientation could mean the difference between life and death in the Belt. I liked living. And twenty years in the Belt had taught me a number of tough lessons in how to keep living. Knowing how to wake up was one of them. When the door responded to my automatic voice command, I was already on my feet, prepared for just about anything.

I wasn't prepared for the tearful six-year-old boy who hurtled directly through the opened door and into my arms.

Anybody would have hugged him. That was

instinctive. Loner or no loner, I had a hysterical child in my arms. I hugged him. And I didn't even have time to question that impulse till hours later, when things had calmed down a bit. I felt a little embarrassed about it then, but what the hell? Nobody'd been there but me and the kid. Nobody saw me.

Beyond the hug, though, I didn't really know what to do. What do you do with a weepy kid? I tried a few awkwardly comforting words and a pat or two. I didn't know whether they were the wanted response, but I felt I ought to do something. I couldn't just stand there like a lump while the kid dripped tears all over both of us.

Fortunately, he was old for his years. And he knew perfectly well that if he didn't tell me what his problem was, I couldn't solve it. In fairly short order he managed to calm himself enough to describe what had happened: when he and Jamin had arrived at their quarters after leaving me, Jamin took his medicine as usual, then settled down for a game of Planets with Collis while they ate their dinner. As Planets so often will, it turned into a time-consuming project that lasted well past dinner. Collis had, he said, been winning. It was past his usual bedtime, but because Jamin wasn't staying long between runs this time, the rules had been relaxed. He would be allowed to stay up till the end of the game.

It was just after telling Collis he could stay up that Jamin collapsed. No warning. No anything. Just one minute he was chatting happily with his son, and the next, he was on the floor.

Collis had tried to revive him, with no success. He

had tried to call his babysitter and got no response either on the phone or at her door. He went back to his own quarters to see if Jamin had recovered in his absence, but no such luck. At last, knowing no other adults on Home Base and not having been briefed on emergency routine, he came to me. "Please," he said pitifully, "I don't know what to do. Papa's never sick. Please help us." As before, when his father admitted how short his visit would be, Collis was doing his best to be brave about it. But he couldn't quite control the trembling of his chin.

"Of course I'll help." I grabbed a tunic with one hand and reached for the phone controls with the other. I got the tunic on and the emergency med-tech number punched in, then had to ask Collis the location of his quarters. Given that, I punched it in, too, and waited just long enough to see the confirmation light on the panel, then followed Collis to his quarters.

Jamin was still there, still sprawled in an awkward heap between the kid's bed and his own. I checked for a pulse, found it, and watched his face while I counted. He was pale as a miner, with a bruised look around the eyes and a sheen of sweat on his forehead and upper lip. The giveaway, though, was the terrible, sweet, familiar smile.

Of course, it wasn't really a smile. It was a physiological reaction, an involuntary tensing of muscles, the reasons for which had been explained to me half a dozen times, always in circumstances such as this, where I wasn't really inclined to listen carefully. I turned to Collis. "Where does he keep his medicine?"

"Here, in this cupboard." He got it out for me, those tear-filled, trusting eyes far too mature, his expression too soberly competent. A child of six should never have to look like that. He glanced uncertainly at his father. "Shouldn't we at least put a pillow under his head, or . . . or something?"

"Don't touch him!" My voice was too sharp. He reacted as to a slap. I wanted to hold him, to make amends, to apologize and explain, but he withdrew behind an aloof indifference so like his father's that I couldn't even try. And I was reminded, with a shock of remembered pain, of myself at his age. That was when I first saw a freefall mutant in gravity shock.

I sat on the edge of a bed, staring at Jamin's medicine bottle to keep from seeing the look in Collis's eyes. The medication must have been tampered with. Collis said Jamin had taken it as required, yet there was no mistaking that terrible smile on Jamin's lips or the sour-sweet odor of his breath when I had leaned over him to take his pulse.

In order to survive the stresses to which normal Earth gravity subjected his freefall-adapted nervous system, a freefall mutant had to have regular doses of a strong medication that altered his metabolic functions and stimulated the production in his system of certain bodily chemicals normal to homozygous gravity dwellers and to heterozygotes, but lacking in the freefall mutant. I didn't know the medical or chemical details, but I was all too familiar with the symptoms of gravity shock. Certainly familiar enough to recognize them when I saw them. My father had suffered it often enough.

I stared at the rock wall beyond the two beds, letting my eyes trace the fault patterns and blast scars left from the original tunneling of Home Base. "I'm sorry I snapped at you, Collis." I had to clear my throat to go on. "It was only that I was frightened. We could hurt him. Badly. Just by moving him. Even by putting a pillow under his head. We have to wait for the med-techs."

He said in a very small, very distant voice, "I shook him, before, when I was trying to wake him."

"It's all right." On impulse I reached across the distance between us. We held hands for a moment, neither of us looking down at the crumpled form on the floor between us. "It's all right. You didn't know. And . . . when the symptoms first . . . that is . . . Probably you didn't hurt him, you know. It wasn't as dangerous then as it would be now."

He was silent for a moment. "Skyrider?"

"Collis?"

"What's the matter with Papa?"

I stared. Could Jamin really never have told him? Fortunately, the med-techs arrived just then. I gave them the medicine bottle and voiced my suspicions. They agreed with my diagnosis, administered a massive dose of the needed medication, and used a portable anti-grav to lift him gently off the floor and trundle him away to Sick Bay. The medicine bottle went with them. They assured me they'd have the remaining contents analyzed.

And that was that. I was left alone with Collis, with nothing more to do except wait. And hope. I think if I'd known how, I might even have prayed.

Collis sat for a long while staring at the door through which his father had been carried away, before he repeated his question. "What's the matter with Papa?"

"Didn't he ever tell you he's a freefall mutant?"

"What's that?"

Sweet space. Now what? "D'you know there are three kinds of people? I mean, space, Collis, you must've been taught that in school. The people who can live on Earth, or in Earth gravity, were the first. . . ."

"Oh, sure; that. I know about that. Those are Grounders, like me. We can live in freefall—" He paused, embarrassed. "I mean we should be able to live in freefall. Most Grounders can, for a whole long time, even. Only they need to get in gravity sometimes." He looked at his feet. "I have to be in it all the time. I have something wrong inside my ear that makes me get spacesick."

"Hey, guy. It's not a crime."

He didn't look up. "I know. But it's embarrassing."

"Well, that's silly. Why be embarrassed about something you can't help, that isn't even your fault anyway?"

He shrugged uncomfortably and took refuge in facts. "They taught us that stuff in school. About Grounders. They're called, um, homo, um, homozyglous—"

"Homozygous."

"Yeah. For gravity. Because everybody has two genes to decide where they can live, and if both genes are the same, you're homozyglous. For gravity, like me, or for freefall, like Papa. Is that what you meant about freefall mutant?"

"That's it. Because the Grounders were first, and after people had been in space quite a while, their genes mutated—changed a little bit, adapting to their new environment—and those new people were called freefall mutants."

"Sure, I had genetics. I just don't always remember all the words. And I don't think my teachers ever said that about freefall mutants. They just said homozyglous." He studied me curiously. "Which are you?"

"I'm the third kind."

"Oh. I forgot. Not homo-anything. One gene for gravity and one for freefall, right? I forget what it's called, though. Except Floaters."

"Because we can 'float' from one environment to the other. We're properly called heterozygotes, which just means we have both genes. But mostly everybody says Floaters."

"It must be neat." He glanced involuntarily at the floor where Jamin had been, and away again. After a silent moment he frowned. "But Mom was like you. A Floater. So how come I'm not?"

"You're forgetting your genetics again. Each parent can give only one of his genes for a given trait. In some things it gets complicated because one trait is dominant, but that's not a problem with the gravity-freefall genes. Your mother had genes for each, but she could only give you one of them. You got the one for gravity. If your biological father was a Grounder, all he had to offer were genes for gravity, and that's what you got. If he was a Floater, you had a two-in-four chance of being a Floater, too. And only a one-in-four chance of being a Grounder. But there you are.''

"Oh." He looked uncertain. Well, I never said I was a teacher. He frowned. "I guess I forgot a lot of genetics. It seemed boring, in school. Will Papa be all right?"

I said, "Yes," with a lot greater certainty than I felt. "Mostly because of your quick thinking. He needed attention right away, and you got it for him."

"He looked awful sick."

"That's because he was. But he'll probably be fine by tomorrow."

It's a long time till tomorrow when you're only six years old. "Would you stay with me till then?" he asked anxiously. And quickly, to allay any suspicions I might have harbored about his courage or lack of it, he added with sublime indifference, "Of course if it's any trouble, you shouldn't bother. A lot of times I stay by myself, when Papa's on a run."

But his papa wasn't on a run.

I didn't know much about kids, but I sure remembered what it felt like to be one. "Sure, kid. I'll stay."

When we were settled for sleep, he reached across the space between beds to hold my hand. If any of the other pilots had seen me then, I'd never have lived it down. The great Skyrider, hotshot babysitter.

But they weren't there to see me, and hell, the kid was scared. He didn't let go my hand all night long.

CHAPTER SEVEN

It was a long night. I didn't sleep particularly well or comfortably: for one thing, I was too aware it was Jamin's bed I was sleeping in, though why that should have mattered so much I don't know; and for another, it wasn't easy finding comfortable positions that left my right arm free to reach across the intervening space to that small, trusting hand.

He didn't seem to have any trouble with it. I had a fleeting, grin-inducing image of him and Jamin holding hands all night every night like that, but on second thought it wasn't really funny. Whether or not it was real, it wasn't funny.

While I waited for Collis to wake in the morning, I had plenty of time to do a little thinking. Just for a change. And plenty to think about: the fight with Lunn and his subsequent flight; the VIP meeting

about the *Marabou*, with the resultant promise of a
Falcon for me; and Jamin's illness. Too much of it
added too well. The VIPs had said that the *Marabou*
was sabotaged. So, apparently, had we been. Whoever did it to the *Marabou* could easily have found
out or even guessed the likeliest candidates to be sent
after her. It was even possible that the military rescue
mission had ended as it had due to sabotage rather
than incompetence. The Patrol's test and rescue pilots didn't tend toward incompetence. And the sabotage could have been something subtle. There was no
guarantee the VIPs would have told us about it even
if they knew, and they might not know.

This was not a happy train of thought. If Lunn had
managed to put me out of action, the Company's
mission might well have been scrubbed. Jamin probably wouldn't be able to dock with the *Marabou* even
if he were willing to try. And I didn't know another
pilot good enough—or dumb enough—to try.

But either the planners hadn't been counting on
Lunn, or they were just naturally thorough, because
Jamin's medicine must have been switched before
Lunn picked that fight with me. Jamin could be
replaced on the mission more readily than I; there
were other Belt pilots who knew how to handle a
liner. Still, the delay in replacing him might have
killed the mission. Anyway, I'd checked his records:
he was the second-best chance for docking, if he
would try it. I thought he would.

It didn't help that he was so damned vulnerable.
Anybody who had access to his medication could kill
him. How many would that be? Two? Three? A

dozen? Start with his med-tech. That would be the first person who knew which batch of medicine was going to Jamin.

Or would it be? Come to think of it, with a chronic condition like Jamin's, the med-techs didn't make the patients go running to Sick Bay every time more medicine was needed. Not unless the prescription was for a controlled substance, and so far, anyway, the Earthers hadn't got officious enough to declare freefall medication controlled substances again. They had done, during the war, and they would again if war broke out again; it was a way of keeping freefall mutants off Earther bases and of keeping track of those who were permitted on Earther bases. Which was only logical, since I'd never met a Faller yet who was pleased to be governed by Grounders. Fallers were all potential, if not actual, Insurrectionists. They had the odd notion that they'd like to have some say in the laws that governed them.

But the war was over; Earth wasn't running scared anymore, and Fallers were permitted the medication to make them able to travel at will within the Belt. Which meant Jamin would have been given an access code, so he could get his medication out of any med-dispenser any time and any place he needed it. The only people who would have access to it, therefore, were people who had access to him or to his quarters.

Jamin and Collis themselves were out of it, obviously. Whom did that leave? Collis had mentioned a babysitter. Did she see him in her quarters or in his? If in his, would Jamin leave his medication in his quarters when he was out on a run? No reason not to, at least on short runs; he had no reason to believe anyone would tamper with it. Which meant the babysitter was at least a possibility.

That was one. How many others? Jamin could easily have a girlfriend, or even a wife or two—though I imagined wives, if any, would have got mentioned in the pilot gossip in the ready room yesterday. That still left girlfriends. A girlfriend is always a good way to get at a man. If Jamin had one, she was first on my list of possibilities. The babysitter was a close second, particularly since she hadn't been available at the crucial time last night when Collis needed her.

I didn't even know whether that in itself was suspicious behavior or just bad luck. I didn't know what sort of agreement Jamin had with her. It might be that she was automatically off duty when he was on Home Base. That would be inconvenient for Jamin, particularly if he did have a girlfriend or two. But even babysitters like to get a little time off now and then, and as Jamin was gone so much of the time, that might have been the only way he could work it.

I dwelt on it for quite a while before I realized I wasn't getting anywhere. My entire list of candidates consisted of a babysitter I'd never met and one or more girlfriends I wasn't sure existed. With any luck, Collis could come up with more possibilities when he woke, so I spent some time trying to think of a way of asking that was innocuous enough not to scare him more than he already was.

I needn't have bothered. As I've said, kids grew

up fast in the Belt. They had to, if they wanted to grow up at all. The first thing Collis asked about when he woke was his father. I hadn't heard from the med-techs, and said so, adding the obvious: that no news was good news at this point. Collis digested that for a moment, dialed himself some breakfast, and introduced the topic of possible medication-switchers while I was still considering delicate ways of mentioning it. He eliminated the girlfriend theory straightaway; Jamin hadn't any. And the babysitter was the only other person Collis knew of who had free access to their quarters whether they were home or not.

We tried to phone her while Collis ate his breakfast and I drank the bland black brew with which the dispenser responded when one dialed coffee. Its only redeeming quality was the caffeine content, which was satisfactorily high and which was what most of us called it; it certainly wasn't coffee. Having been raised on it, most of us were satisfied with it till the first time we tasted contraband coffee from Earth. After that we tolerated it.

The phone screen remained blank, though we let it ring so often that the computer finally got miffed about it and asked whether we might not be wiser to try again later. We decided it would be more direct, if not altogether sensible, to go ring her door chimes. If she was refusing to answer the phone, she would probably not answer the door either, but at least it gave us the illusion of positive action. We needed to do something.

First, though, I dialed Sick Bay to ask about Jamin.

A med-clerk with an offended face told me Jamin was "doing as well as could be expected."

"That's nice," I said. "How well is that?"

His face got more offended. "If you wish to obtain more detailed information as to the patient's condition at this time, you'll have to speak directly with his med-tech."

"Fine. Connect me."

"I'm sorry, but I can't do that at this time."

He didn't look sorry, but I let it go. "Why not?"

"Med-Tech Kurasaki is assisting in surgery at this time."

"Wonderful. Can you at least tell me when Jamin will be released?"

"I'm afraid that information is not available at this time."

"Then can you tell me what time that information will be available?"

"Not at this time."

"When will Kurasaki be available?"

"Med-Tech Kurasaki has a very busy schedule. I'm afraid I can't—"

"I know. You can't tell me at this time."

"That is correct." His face had gone past offended, right into civilly outraged. At this time.

"Were you ever six years old?"

That threw him. "I beg your pardon?"

"There's a six-year-old boy here who's waiting for information about his father. Like whether he'll be all right. And when he'll be coming home. That sort of thing. The information that you don't have 'at this time.' He hasn't got anybody else, and he and his

father are hell of close. I just had a fleeting notion
that if you'd ever been six, and could still remember
what it was like, maybe that information might pry a
little cooperation out of you. But I can tell by looking
that you probably were never six.'' His face had been
undergoing a nasty series of expressions, culminating
in ugly. ''And if you were, you probably didn't have
a father. Forget I asked. Maybe I'll call back later.
Like when you're out to lunch. From a computer I
might get a little human empathy.'' I cut the connection before he could figure out what to do with his
face. I'd seen more of it than I really wanted to.

Beside me, Collis was giggling. ''Sometimes I
sure wish I could talk to clerks that way.''

I grinned at him. ''Better wait till you've got rank
on them. They can make too much trouble, otherwise.''

''I know.'' He sobered. ''Besides, Papa says I
should always treat them nice because they're people,
too.''

''Sometimes I wonder.''

''Me too.''

''But your papa's right. They are people, and people do react better to kindness than to insults.''

''That guy wouldn't have.''

''Let's go see your sitter.'' I was getting out of my
depth, and I knew it. This kid needed competent
adult companionship and guidance. Not a hotshot
Skyrider with antisocial tendencies.

Unfortunately, he wasn't going to get any adult
companionship and guidance from that sitter anymore.
I had a feeling, when her door indicated willingness
to open without a voice command from within, that I

111

shouldn't have brought Collis with me. I was right. The sitter was dead.

She had been very young and very pretty. Her quarters betrayed her Earther origin: since she lived in pilot territory, the rooms were naked rock furnished in metal and plastic, but she had hung bright fabric draperies on the walls and covered every flat surface with cloth or fur, even the seats of the chairs. The dispenser in the center of the dining table sported an odd little stitched fabric cover designed apparently in the misguided hope of disguising it. A genuine glass container beside it held a riotous collection of bright plastic flowers and dusty greenery.

The most poignant object, though, was an open-topped metal cylinder on the floor near the disposal chute. I didn't recognize it at once, and would never have if I hadn't been to Earth: it was a wastebasket. On Earth, people collected their refuse in containers such as that. When the containers were full, they carried them to similar larger containers outside their dwellings, from which the contents were collected at regular intervals by persons who then trucked the refuse to the nearest recycling center.

She must have known or been told before she spaced out for the Belt that every shuttle, every inhabited asteroid, and every chamber on the larger asteroids had at least one disposal chute and usually more than one. Refuse went through the chutes and directly into the recycling facilities without need of the distance transport required on Earth. Yet she had brought that thing with her, despite the weight and space limitations necessarily set on immigrants' luggage, and despite its ugliness and its absolute superfluousness she had neither discarded it on arrival nor relegated it to concealment in a cupboard or to a use other than its intended one. She placed it exactly where the designers of her quarters had known a disposal would be wanted, beneath the wall disposal they had supplied, where it stood as a prominent reminder of the many great and subtle differences between her native land and her chosen home.

I admired her for that odd little gesture of identity. For the most part, her taste in chamber decoration was at least moderately repellant to me, but I could understand the impulse that must have prompted her to bring that object with her and the stubborn defiance that kept her from relinquishing or hiding it after she was settled.

Collis hung back when I moved on past the table and into her bedchamber, and I was glad of it when I saw her. Not that she was an unattractive sight even in death; she lay in careful beauty, her auburn hair spread like a halo on the pillow around her pale face, which had a gentle expression of mild surprise. She wore a fragile nightgown of some lavender fabric so light and delicate that its hem, where it hung off the bed, moved in the air disturbed by our arrival. Her hands were primly folded over her breast in a gesture evocative of innocence. I had a vague impression that on Earth, where the dead were treated with startling reverence and often buried whole, this was a pose in which the corpse was put for viewing (though why anyone would wish to view the dead I didn't quite understand). It was as though her assassin, having performed his unpleasant task, had wished in some way to apologize.

Little attempt had been made to conceal the manner of her death; there were bruises on her neck where the arteries had been crushed—a relatively quick and quiet way to kill an unresisting victim. She could not have done that to herself. Yet there was no sign of a struggle. Either she had been willing, which was difficult to believe but possible, or she had been drugged.

Still, it was a neat and orderly death, and she was a neat and orderly corpse. The only reason I wanted to keep Collis from seeing her or from observing her closely was that I didn't know Jamin's attitude toward death and the dead. I had found no general topic more delicate than that—not even sex, on strait-laced Earth. People who would eagerly view pornographic holofilms were offended at mention of death or at "inappropriate" attitudes toward death. I had no wish to offend either Jamin or Collis by expressing a different attitude from theirs or by behaving in a way Jamin might consider unseemly.

Collis seemed to take the situation well. He knew at once that the sitter was dead, and I didn't try to hide her or the fact of her death; that could surely only make the situation more alarming to him if he had been taught to fear death with an Earther passion. I did, however, get him out of there as soon as I reasonably could. We phoned Sick Bay from his quarters, not hers.

Since it was a different department, we didn't get the med-clerk I'd talked to before, which was as well. I reported what we'd found and told them where to look for us if they needed us. Collis was too quiet, but otherwise normal. I still couldn't get any information from Sick Bay about Jamin, and I didn't know what to do with the kid. I knew he needed something to take his mind off. So I took him where I went when that was what I needed: the pilots' rec room.

Magda, Tomsaunders, Roul, and Chekov were there, playing Planets for malite markers and happily insulting one another between moves. There were some short-runners at another table, but I didn't know any of them, and after some startled glances at Collis they ignored us. I took him to the group I knew and pulled up chairs for both of us.

"Got a new job?" asked Tomsaunders, glancing at Collis.

"Not the one you mean," I said. "You want something to drink, Collis?"

Magda looked up from the chips she was counting. "That Jamin's kid?"

"You know my father?" asked Collis.

Magda grinned. "I wiped his nose for him last night, after he tangled with the Skyrider."

Collis looked at me. "You and Papa fought?"

"Um," I said. "Fruit juice, maybe? Or a soda?"

"Your move, Chekov," said Roul.

"Listen, you guys, I need a favor," I said.

"Soda," said Collis.

"Most of us do," said Tomsaunders.

"Where's Jamin, anyway?" asked Magda.

"Your move," said Roul.

115

"He's in Sick Bay," said Collis. "He got gravity-shocked."

"I made my move," said Chekov, "and raised you ten."

"What move?" said Roul. "I don't see a move."

"Is he okay?" asked Magda.

"That's because you're looking in the wrong quadrant, rock head," said Tomsaunders. "Magda, you're up."

"I think so," I said. "They won't tell us anything over the phone, but Collis got help there in time, last night. Go ahead and dial a soda, Collis. Tomsaunders, will you listen? This is important. I really do need a favor."

When they got involved in Planets, they really got involved. But I managed to pry them loose long enough to explain my situation. I'd already called the flight deck and found out my Falcon was there. When I got to that part, they were all amazed I'd had the patience to explain the rest.

"Go for it," said Roul.

"I can't; the kid needs a sitter."

"I can take care of myself," said Collis.

"It's considered polite to lower your glass from your lips while speaking," I said.

He lowered his glass. "You don't have to worry about me. I spend a lot of time alone when Papa's on a run."

"Well, you shouldn't," said Magda.

"Not healthy," said Tomsaunders.

"Do you play Planets?" asked Chekov.

"Sure, Papa and I play all the time. But what are all those little piles of square things?"

"Malite chips," said Chekov at the same time as I said, "Nothing important." Chekov looked at me in surprise. "Skyrider, what—"

Magda and Tomsaunders were looking at me in disbelief. "You aren't going to," began Tomsaunders.

Magda interrupted, her tone aggrieved. "It's no fun with nothing at stake!"

I couldn't argue with all three of them. When I left, they had already begun to explain to Collis the finer points of betting on each move in a game of Planets. But I'd salved my uncertain sense of propriety by insisting that they switch from malite chips to chocolate. There were a few mild complaints, but it didn't seem to slow the game once they got started again. When I glanced back from the doorway, Chekov was leaning intently over the board, explaining some complex strategy to Collis, who was listening with equal intensity, his face clear of shadows once more.

Tomsaunders was leaning back, studying his game pieces . . . and absent-mindedly nibbling his stake.

CHAPTER EIGHT

The Earthers I'd known tended to think of shuttles in terms of sleek, aerodynamically streamlined vessels designed to slice through the heavy atmosphere of Earth or Mars with grace, beauty, and impunity. Liners were off-loaded by such needle-nosed, heat-shielded shuttles, and those were what Earthers saw. But in the Belt, most shuttles were boxy, graceless objects meant to cut through no atmosphere but that of a flight deck and never through the buffeting winds of a planet. They were unwieldy-looking things, quicker than they seemed and sturdy enough to withstand the occasional collision with a wild rock or two; reliable as all hell; and ugly as sin. No romance. No personality. No sex appeal. They looked like what they were: trucks. Big, bulky, dependable trucks.

Mind you, a person can learn to love a truck.

There is a certain beauty in the plain sturdiness of them. And a tool that looks like a tool is usually more reliable and almost always more beautiful than a tool disguised as something it isn't. Form that fits function is often the most attractive as well as the most effective design.

But a person can drive a truck and wish for a Starbird. Or for a Falcon. A person can wield a butcher knife and wish for a sword. I had my sword. My Falcon. Waiting on the flight deck, as sleek and slim and elegant as any shuttle that ever nosed a hole through Earth's stormy atmosphere or glided out over the gleaming deserts of Mars.

She was delicate and fragile as the bird she was named for—and as deadly. She could do a truck's work. She was built for it, and she could take it. But she could dance on atmosphere in her spare time, and she was built for that, too. Falcons were the fastest and most maneuverable shuttles ever built, and they looked it. Their design was based on several technological breakthroughs made by the military during the Colonial Incident. They were capable of greater speed and distances on less fuel than any other space vessel made. Only the military's tiny Starbird could outmaneuver a Falcon, and even a Starbird couldn't outdistance one.

It would take the Patrol a hell of a lucky shot to catch me now. When I saw her waiting for me on the flight deck, I just stared at her in absolute wonder for a while. She wasn't the first Falcon I'd ever seen, but she was the first I'd ever owned. And she was all mine. Every clean, sweeping curve of that hull; every ounce of steel and plastic; every centimeter of filter and coil—she was mine. And I was in love.

I'd been staring at her for a good five minutes before I realized I had company. Granger was off flight control duty, but he'd come down to the flight deck anyway, to see me take possession of my new toy. When I finally noticed him standing beside me, he grinned. "She's a beauty."

"She sure as hell is." I felt like a kid at Christmas.

"Gonna take her out?"

That brought me back to reality fast enough. "Not till I've been over her with a decon kit, right down to the rivets in her pretty tail."

"Decon?" He stared. "What do you think she's contaminated with? She just came from Alpha Seven. What could she have caught there?"

"Sudden death." I told him about Lunn and Jamin and the babysitter. "Somebody doesn't want us to make this run. I didn't ask the VIPs what payload the *Marabou* is carrying. But either it's damned important, or the political extremists have decided to make an issue of it anyway, for some reason. To prove, I suppose, whatever it is extremists usually hope to prove by killing innocents."

"You never seemed innocent to me." He grinned.

"I meant the passengers on the *Marabou*, rock head. I'm just a side issue; I might get in the way." I looked again at my new shuttle. "Me and my Falcon." The sheer delight of saying "my Falcon" made me grin, but I sobered when I thought what might have been done to her. "By God, they'd better not hurt her. I'll kill them."

Granger grinned again. "It's okay to send Lunn after you with a force blade and a babysitter after Jamin with fake medication. It's even okay to murder the babysitter. You'll put up with all that. But not if they touch your Falcon."

In the fraction of a second it took me to realize how dumb it would be to slug him, I saw him brace himself. He should have known I'd see the humor. But I did have a reputation for hitting first and thinking later. "Well, hell." I smiled at my earnestness and shrugged. "We don't know for sure that the babysitter is connected with all this. It is all guesswork. Though I admit I can't think of any other reasonable explanation for any of it." I looked at my Falcon. "Anyway, all those things are different." That didn't sound right, either. "Space, you know what I mean. Everything except switching Jamin's medicine . . ."

"I know." And he did; he was a Belter, too. We had the same values. Of course we didn't consider a Falcon more valuable than a human life. But there was a matter of principle. People can fight back. Unmanned equipment can't.

Danger, even from each other, was something we accepted, and lived with—or died of. But one didn't tamper with the equipment. That wasn't a law; it wasn't even a rule. It was, and had to be, a fact of life. We lived in artificial environments, and we had to depend on them. One act of carelessness or of sabotage to our life-support systems could have such far-ranging effects that to perform such an act, either by neglect or by intention, had to be absolutely beyond the realm of acceptable behavior.

Mistake were made from time to time. That was unavoidable. I'd made one myself, and killed a man, and spent a considerable time afterward trying, in various unconscious ways, to kill myself before I learned how to live with what I'd done. That had been an accident caused by neglect. To kill a man by such means, intentionally . . . Well, I would never have learned how to forgive myself for that.

The Belt wouldn't have got colonized in the first place without the tacit agreement among the colonizers that the equipment was sacred. You could attack a man, but you didn't attack his environment. Unless there was a war. In war, even the laws of nature get mucked with, and the laws of man don't stand a chance. Sabotage was common then.

Nor was it unthinkable in war or in peace to try to shoot a shuttle out from under its pilot. That was much like attacking the pilot himself; he had a chance to shoot back. But the shuttle couldn't defend itself when the pilot wasn't in it. And the idea of sabotaging it, so the shuttle itself would kill its passengers, was repugnant. People were vulnerable enough to begin with, and the more so in space. There were a hell of a lot more ways to kill a man than there were to conceive one.

Maybe if we were tougher creatures we'd have made less fuss about the sanctity of our life-support systems. But we were puny little out-of-place air-breathers trying to make it in a near-vacuum, and we had freefall mutations to complicate things and Grounders who had to have their gravity fixes, and overall we were just plain scared. Which probably explained

all the fighting and rough acting we were so prone to;
nobody likes to admit he's scared.

Anyway, that Falcon was going to be my life-
support system for some time to come, and I'd have
gone over her before the mission in any event since I
was pretty fond of living. But I'd be a lot more
thorough with the thought of possible sabotage in
mind. I didn't know who was behind the attempts on
my life and Jamin's, but whoever was after us, he,
she, or they had made a mistake in using Jamin's
medication. I might not even have considered the
possibility of sabotage to my Falcon if it hadn't been
for that. People just didn't do things like that: we
weren't at war. If you wanted to kill somebody, you
killed him. You didn't muck about with *things*.

Somebody had mucked about with Jamin's medicine.
And the same somebody who did that might muck
about with my Falcon. The *Marabou* was different.
She was a big ship, and she'd been treated fairly;
only her engines and her pilots were harmed. On a
big ship the life-support systems were separate from
the drive. On the *Marabou* they would continue to
function till her passengers and crew were dead.
Whoever planned that had political savvy. If Jamin
and I were unsuccessful, the passengers would be
just as dead and the payload would be just as lost as
if the whole liner had been destroyed. But only Earth's
laws would have been broken. Colonists wouldn't be
angered by that. They didn't care much for Earth
laws anyway.

Jamin's medicine had been an iffy thing. It was
too much like damaging life support. And that was

the strongest taboo in the Belt. The person who would switch medications might meddle with a shuttle, and on a ship that small, life-support systems were integral with everything else. A threat to the integrity of the ship was a threat to the life support. I couldn't afford to take any chances.

Besides, she was my Falcon. Mine. And while the thought of a sabotaged life-support system filled me with righteous indignation, the thought of somebody damaging my own personal Falcon was worse.

Hell, I hadn't even flown her yet!

I spent most of the day conducting an arduous examination of my new shuttle from nose to tail, cockpit to exhaust, wingtip to wingtip, till I knew her better than I knew the back of my hand. I also knew, when I was finished, that we were indeed up against somebody who played dirty. Very dirty.

There was a device in the air-filter coils that looked so much like a new roll of filter material that it would have passed the average inspection as it was designed to clog the system by degrees. We wouldn't have blown our top. We'd just have been asphyxiated so slowly we probably wouldn't even have known what was happening until far too late to do anything about it.

Then, in the dispenser controls, I found a printed circuit that was just fine except for one thing: it was printed of nonconducting plastics. They looked just like the conducting plastics that should have been there, and I discovered the difference by accident. It was a circuit that controlled the water-recycling unit, and it wasn't one for which I would have carried a spare.

Last, but certainly not least, I found a rivet in the engine that wasn't set quite right. Maybe that was the one I was meant to find if I looked for any. Maybe somebody thought if I found a rivet that revealed a neat little time bomb, I'd deactivate it and think we were safe. It's even possible I would have, if I hadn't found the other two devices first. But I had, and the rivet made me nervous all over again. I went back over the whole ship just to make sure I hadn't missed any other interesting rivets, nuts, bolts, or similar subterfuge.

By the time I was done, I felt I could have built a Falcon blindfolded if I'd been given the parts. And I was confident that there was nothing further wrong with mine. She needed a few minor additions and adjustments that the original designer had overlooked, probably because she didn't have smuggling in mind when she designed the cargo holds and left out the weaponry. I wanted weapons, extra sealant racks, and a little work on the larger cargo hold that I would have to do myself since I wouldn't want the Company to know all the details. But aside from those deficiencies, my sweet Falcon was clean and in good repair.

Now I had to keep her that way. Which meant asking for help from people I ordinarily hadn't much use for: Company-loyal Earther personnel. I needed a constant and careful guard on her until we lifted off on our mission, and that was the only group from which I could draw enough people and be sure I wasn't getting one or more of "the enemy"—whoever the enemy was.

It seemed logical, at the time, to assume that Company-loyal Earthers could not be guilty of sabotaging the *Marabou* or her would-be rescuers. Which only proves that logic isn't everything.

CHAPTER NINE

I got the guards situated to my satisfaction, and called Sick Bay to see how Jamin was doing. They told me they'd turned him loose. I didn't even stop to clean up; he'd want to know where Collis was, and Collis would want to know Jamin was okay. That seemed more urgent than getting the engine dust off my hands. I made a dash for the rec room.

But Jamin had already tracked down his son. Magda, Tomsaunders, Roul, and Chekov were still at the gaming table where I'd left them. Collis was with them, wearing a soda-foam mustache and a stubborn expression. Jamin was hovering over him, as arrogant and overbearing as ever. The bruised look remained under his eyes, but that was the only sign of last night's ordeal. He glanced around when Collis grinned a greeting at me, and if looks could kill, I'd have died. But then, if looks could kill, I'd have been dead a long time before that.

"What in space did you think you were doing, leaving a six-year-old boy in a room full of gambling pilots? Do you know what they've been doing? They've been teaching my son to gamble! At Planets! They've been here the whole afternoon, gambling with him!"

I walked right up to Collis and put my hand on the back of his chair. It took some doing, but I met Jamin's gaze without looking guilty. "Hello, Jamin. Sick Bay told me they'd let you out. I'm happy to see you're so well recovered. Better than ever, in fact: arrogant, ungrateful, unpleasant, irritating, and ugly. I'm glad your illness didn't have any lasting effect."

"Gambling," he said. "Did you hear me? They've been—"

"Don't bother to thank me. I'm always happy to help out a fellow pilot in trouble. How was your afternoon, Collis?"

He gestured toward the stacks of chocolate before him. "I've been winning. See?" He grinned.

So did the other pilots. So did I. And so, reluctantly, did Jamin. "You don't plan to eat all that at once, I hope?" he asked his son.

"No," Collis said seriously. "I've been thinking about that, and I think it might make me sick, don't you?"

"I certainly do."

"Tomsaunders, you're eating your bet again," said Collis.

"Stake," said Tomsaunders. "It's called your stake when it's in front of you, and—"

"—it's not a bet till you put it out here," said Collis. "I know, I just forgot for a minute." He looked reprovingly at Tomsaunders. "You're still eating it."

"Oh. Yeah." Tomsaunders looked at the square of chocolate in his hand, started to put it down, then looked at Jamin and shrugged. "Guess it doesn't matter, if you're going to close down the game."

"I'm taking Collis out of it, if that's what you mean." Jamin was working at recovering his anger. He glared at me again. "He shouldn't have been here in the first place. What were you doing while these—these—"

"Degenerates," suggested Magda.

"—were teaching my son—"

"I was taking time bombs off my Falcon."

That shut him up. It shut up everybody except Collis, who brightened visibly. "Why did you have bombs on your Falcon?" he asked.

I looked at Jamin. He blinked. I smiled. It wasn't a friendly smile. I wasn't feeling friendly. I'd been in an agony of worry for Jamin, held his kid's hand the whole long night, found babysitters so I could clean booby traps off the shuttle that would otherwise have killed us tomorrow, and for thanks I got a lecture on the care and feeding of six year olds. If he'd been a Floater I'd have torn him apart. As it was, I damn near did it anyway when he responded to Collis's question by asking where his babysitter was. Was that all he could think about?

I let the kid answer. "She's dead. She didn't

answer her phone last night, so this morning we went to her quarters—''

''Who's 'we'?'' Jamin asked suspiciously.

''The Skyrider an' me,'' said Collis. ''We tried to call her when we woke up, and when she still didn't answer, we—''

Jamin was staring at me. ''Collis spent the night with *you*?''

''There are worse fates, I expect.''

''She stayed with me, Papa. I asked her to, and she—''

Embarrassment can be a real deterrent to anger, particularly when fighting, which would otherwise be quite a satisfactory outlet for both emotions, is off-limits. I said quickly, ''It's no big deal. The kid was worried about you, and we couldn't get hold of the sitter. Listen, I pulled three booby traps off my Falcon, and they were pretty damn good ones. We'll have to be careful—''

''Amalie's *dead*?'' asked Jamin.

At least I'd kept Collis from blurting details of our night to all these pilots. Having stayed with him was something I could live down. Having held his hand I wasn't so sure about. Anxiety over that slowed my thinking. ''Who?'' I asked, frowning.

''Amalie. My sitter,'' said Collis.

''Oh. Sure.'' I looked at Jamin again. ''Murdered, apparently, though there was no sign of a struggle and I haven't heard from Ground Patrol since I reported what we found. She couldn't have crushed her own carotid arteries. But why wouldn't she struggle?''

''I don't know.'' His tone said he didn't much

care, either. "The important thing is, what'll we do now? Collis has to have a sitter."

"Murder, mayhem, booby traps, and time bombs, and you're worried about finding a babysitter?" To my relief, the other pilots seemed to have lost interest in us and were setting up a new game of Planets. With chips, this time. "Space, there must be hundreds of them on this rock. Call Central and order one up."

"Just order up a random babysitter." He sounded like I'd suggested rocks for dinner.

"Sure. Why not?"

"Have you any idea how important a babysitter is in a child's life?"

I shrugged. "I know you have to have one."

"Damn straight, he has to have one. And we're talking about a person with whom he'll spend every waking hour till you and I get back from this crazy run. A person who'll influence his every attitude and decision. You think I can turn that kind of responsibility over to just any random stranger? For space sake, look what happened today!"

"Yeah. Awful. The kid won a bunch of chocolate. Fate worse than death, and that. Probably scarred his psyche for life." I grinned at Collis. And saw the worry in his eyes. He'd forestalled one fight by displaying his winnings, and here we were headed for another. The kid was looking for another hole card. He'd just found out how fragile his father was, and it looked like he might have his lifework cut out for him, trying to keep Jamin out of fights.

I remembered what Jamin had said last night about

me playing macho with my fists and felt my grin falter. To the kid, I said, "How the hell he's survived this long I don't know, but we'll keep him going for a while yet. Don't worry so hard, kid." To Jamin, I said, "Let's get out of here. If finding a babysitter is so damned important, you'd better get started."

"You could take me with," said Collis.

"Why d'you think I'm helping gather up your winnings? Did you think we were going to leave you here?" I asked.

"I meant you could take me with, on your run," said Collis. "Then Papa wouldn't have to find a sitter for me before you can go."

"No, Collis," said Jamin.

"Sorry, kid," I said. "Look, Jamin—"

"But I want to go," said Collis.

"No," said Jamin.

I happened to be looking at the kid when Jamin said that. I saw the disappointment . . . and the rebellion. Then he noticed me watching him, and the rebellious look increased as he lifted his chin to stare me down. I'd seen that look somewhere before. Like maybe in mirrors. "You really can't go, Collis," I said. "We'll be in freefall the whole way."

The chin lifted a fraction higher. "Why?"

"Because it saves fuel we might need for maneuvering," said Jamin, his tone of voice quite final.

That wasn't strictly true, since I was having some changes made in the Falcon that I hadn't told Jamin about and didn't intend to, but it quelled Collis. Briefly. When he'd thought about it for a moment, he said, "Maybe I wouldn't be sick in freefall like I used to."

"Collis," said Jamin.

"Look, kid," I said.

"I know," said Collis. "I can't go. It's grownup stuff." That stubborn chin lifted again, and the blue eyes flashed. "I don't care. Just you guys better not fight with each other, that's all."

"I said I'd keep him alive, didn't I?" I said.

Collis wasn't listening, though. He looked thoughtful. "If there's medicine to make you comfortable in gravity, Papa, why isn't there medicine to make me comfortable in freefall?"

"There isn't any medicine to—"

Jamin cut me off. "I don't know, son."

I stared. I'd been about to tell Collis the truth: that his father wasn't comfortable in gravity. He could survive it for a while, but not in comfort. Now that Collis knew the danger of gravity shock, I suppose I assumed Jamin would tell him the whole truth. I was wrong.

"I don't know, either," said Collis. He was watching me. And there was that light in his eyes again. Jamin might not tell his son everything, but the kid was a quick learner. He looked like he'd already guessed a lot more than Jamin wanted him to know. Asking about the medicine had been a test of some sort, and Jamin had failed it. The boy who knew enough to create a diversion when it looked like his father was going to start a fight was not a boy who would be easily fooled by half-truths or awkward lies. He must have been questioning them for a long time now. And last night had supplied a lot of answers.

I thought he was trying to tell me something, but I couldn't guess what. He'd looked at me, not his father, when he asked about medicines. And he was watching me, still. I said, "Collis . . ."

Jamin interrupted again. "What are you doing to protect that Falcon while we're not with it?"

"I've put a full-time guard on it. All Earth-loyal Company men. Grounders, mostly. Whoever's behind all this, it's got to be Insurrectionists. It doesn't make sense, otherwise." Which shows how politically naive I was.

CHAPTER TEN

We were all politically naive in those days. Jamin accepted my logic without question. I left him and Collis at their quarters and went on to mine, where I sat down at the phone console to order up all the supplies I could imagine we might possibly need on the mission. That included a number of things the Company and the Patrol wouldn't much like, not all of which I could install myself; but I figured if I moved fast enough, I could have it all done before anybody official thought to question what I was requisitioning or what the workers were doing with it.

It was a long night. I had the dispenser overhauled and supplied with twice what we might reasonably expect to need. I had new sealant racks installed in every chamber, complete with bottles of sealant and a couple of cases of spares; ever since the accident that killed Django, I'd been a little obsessed with sealant. If I'd had it on that run, it wouldn't have saved him, but few obsessions are logical.

I had a pair of powerful energy weapons installed, and a deflector shield that would ward off anything short of a direct hit from the Patrol's energy weapons. Somebody was awake when I ordered that; I was told the Company wouldn't pay. "Install them anyway," I said. "Charge it to Jamin and me." At least nobody questioned our credit rating.

Meantime, I was overhauling the cargo holds to my own satisfaction. Few of the changes I made would be necessary on the *Marabou* run, but the refurbishing that was necessary for that made a good screen for my own activities. Extra bulkhead plates, paid for by the Company, came in with the other supplies, and nobody asked what I needed them for. I made sure nobody was present when I used them. We were increasing my Falcon's fuel capacity, and that necessitated quite a bit of remodeling and the loss of half a cargo compartment. Nobody noticed when the other half, and half of an adjoining compartment, disappeared with it. If we survived the *Marabou* run, I was going to have the best-equipped smuggling shuttle in the Belt.

She needed a name. I had a lot of time to think about that while I was riveting in my false bulkhead. Of course, she had a string of identification numbers already, but if I registered her with a real name straightaway, those numbers would never be used again outside the computer files. However, though

I'd long dreamed of owning a Falcon, I'd considered the possibility of getting one so remote that I hadn't thought what I'd name her.

That may sound like a trivial matter, but it wasn't trivial to me. That Falcon was going to be my primary home, if I had a home, for some time to come. Her name, not mine, would register us at every flight deck, every landing site, and in every flight computer. Her name, like the *Sunjammer* and the *Big Eagle*, would outlive the mistakes of her pilot. If she outlived me, as she would if I piloted her well, the name I had given her would remain as a reminder of what I had stood for, what I had accomplished, and what I had believed. Maybe even what I had fought for, if this *Marabou* incident turned out, as I had begun to fear it might, to be the first battle in the second Colonial War.

Of course, in a war, she would have less chance of outliving me. But although I had the usual human desire for even a sideways hint of immortality, I wasn't really as concerned with what would happen after I died as I was with what happened while I was still around. Either way, this Falcon would be identified with me and I with her, and I wanted her to have a name I'd be comfortable with.

By morning I'd considered and discarded two or three dozen possibilities. And I'd got my false bulkhead neatly in place, with its concealed hatch convincingly masquerading as just an ordinary group of plasteel bulkhead plates. The release control was in the galley, grouped with the new dispenser systems check switches, where it was unlikely to be discovered even in a Patrol-sponsored inspection.

The weapons I had installed would have been illegal if I'd called them weapons when I ordered them up. But the same equipment can be used for blasting wild rocks as for blasting a Patrol ship. Our quickest route to the *Marabou* would take us back past New England, through the same wild rocks that I'd blamed for my shuttle damage the day before. I used that to justify both the weapons and the deflector shield. The Company wasn't about to balk at much of anything I asked for just then. They accepted my prevarications without a word. They still refused to pay, but we had credit and plenty of time to find a way to get the charge canceled.

Jamin arrived on the flight deck in time to watch the changing of the guard as the night watch ended. The new group, as Company-oriented and Earth-loyal as the men they replaced, glared covertly at Jamin and me as they took up their stations. They weren't any more pleased to be guarding a shuttle for me than I was to need them. My failure to fight in the war had put me on the wrong side of everybody. Insurrectionists regarded me as a potential Earth loyalist, and the Earth loyalists regarded me as a potential Insurrectionist. Both sides regarded me as a coward, and potentially a spy, which isn't as contradictory as it might seem at first glance. Neither side trusted me, though both knew I ran a lot of supplies for freelancers and homesteaders, which should logically have reassured the Insurrectionists. Part of the reason it didn't was that I didn't let it; I didn't want to be trusted. I still didn't want to choose sides. As long as I could, I wanted to stay defiantly independent of both.

But I really knew which side I'd choose if I had to, and I glared as bitterly at my new guards as they glared at me. In the last few years the Company stance had really become indefensible. Outlawing supply runs to freelancers and homesteaders had been the final straw. And breaking that law had been my first open defiance of Earth government in the Belt.

Jamin was staring at my Falcon. "What in space have you done?" he asked.

"Refitted her for the mission," I said. "What bothers you about that?"

"Who paid for the weapons?"

Naturally, the first thing he'd ask about would be the one thing I hadn't been able to con the Company into supplying free of charge. "We did."

He stared. "*We?* I don't know whether I ought to ask. . . . Who's 'we'?"

"You and me. Who else?"

"That's what I was afraid of."

"Did you find a sitter for Collis?"

"My God, Melacha, we'll be paying for this for the rest of our lives!"

"We may not live that long. Did you find a sitter?"

"Yes. How much did it cost?"

"What, the weapons?"

"Yes, the weapons! What else would I ask about?" He looked at me, suddenly suspicious. "What else did I help pay for?"

141

"Nothing, exactly. I mean, it's sort of all part of the same system."

"What is?"

"Don't menace me like that, or I'll knock your arrogant face in."

"What else did I help pay for?"

"Just the deflector shield."

"Deflector shield!"

"That's it. Great thing to have when you run up against . . . a flurry of wild rocks."

"Or the Patrol, right?"

Three guards looked our way; he was raising his voice. "Be quiet," I said. "Why would we run up against the Patrol? We're on a Company mission."

"Not we. You. After the *Marabou* run." He started walking around my Falcon, surveying the visible changes in her. "My God. Weapons, deflector shield; what the hell are you outfitting for? A mission, or a war?"

Two more guards looked our way. "Damn it, shut up before I shut you up. If you keep on, we'll have a war right here on the flight deck. Is that what you want?"

"Sweet space." He was still staring at the Falcon. "Lasers or photars?"

"Both. Look, Jamin . . ."

"Both! Are you serious? You've installed—"

"Both. Jamin, listen to me. If you want to argue about this, we can go to the ready room and argue. Otherwise, I'm serious about this: if you don't shut the hell up, I will shut you up. The only reason I haven't done it already is that you're a Faller, but you can't hide behind that forever.''

He caught me by surprise. I admit it. I wasn't even looking at him when he swung; I was looking at the guards, wondering how much of this they could hear and what they'd make of it. Jamin's fist connected with my chin and knocked me silly, and I hadn't even seen it coming.

If I had, I might have ducked it. And if I'd ducked it, I might have had sense enough to pull my punches when I hit him back. As it was, I didn't have time to think about that. I completely forgot he was a Faller. The idiot. The only chance he had was to knock me out with the first blow. When he missed that, he risked his life. And I damn near took it.

I had him on the floor, with a broken jaw that I'd have broken twice if I hadn't broken my hand the first time, before I remembered who and what he was. "Oh, space. Oh, *damn* you!" I said, cradling my broken hand in my other arm. "Are you all right? I might have killed you, you space-happy rock brain!''

He actually tried to hit me again. But the med-techs had arrived by then, and they saved the pride of us both by pulling us apart with a great show of difficulty. I didn't let them lead me away till I knew Jamin was all right. He made a token effort to hit me again. I responded with an ineffectual lurch in his direction, knowing full well the med-techs would stop me before I could get close to him.

It was a fine performance, except for the minor problem that I couldn't keep a straight face all the way through it. I burst out laughing, and after a moment Jamin grinned painfully in response. "I think you broke my damn jaw," he said.

"I know I broke my damn hand. Come on, let's get to Sick Bay. It's another stupid delay. . . . Why the *hell* did you hit me?"

"Because you said—"

"I know what I said. But damn, Jamin, I might have killed you."

"Do you still think I'm hiding behind . . . I mean . . . Did I ever even tell you what I was?" His words were slurred, and he put a hand delicately to his swelling jaw.

"No. I shouldn't have said that. Okay?"

The med-techs were watching us, ready to pull us apart again if need be. Jamin looked at them, looked at me, and achieved another crooked grin. "Okay. Peace. Let's get to Sick Bay; the VIPs are waiting for us, for a final briefing."

"Let them wait." I glanced back at the Falcon. "It would cost more to have the weapons removed than it did to have them installed. You don't really want—"

"It's okay, hotshot. You can keep your damn weapons. I'll even pay my share without grumbling. Just don't hit me again, okay?" He grinned ruefully.

"Okay. As long as you don't hit me first again."

"Did you really break your hand?"

"Did I really break your jaw?"

We grinned at each other like the idiots we were.

"You'd better get to Sick Bay," said one of the med-techs.

"Oh, right." We went, still grinning whenever we

looked at each other. This was more like it. If Jamin could keep acting human, we might yet be friends. Which would be as well if we were going to spend the next few weeks in close contact with each other on the *Marabou* run.

Sick Bay mended us, the med-techs grumbling as always. Jamin's jaw was no problem, but they complained that I'd broken my hand one time too many. They couldn't get all the fingers to work right. I told them to do the best they could in the time I had, and they told me how important it was that I come back as soon as I had more time so they could spend a few hours doing it over again right. I said I would; I'd be right back in as soon as I had some time, but not today. They complained some more and let me go.

The VIPs had no new information; they just didn't want to let us set out without having a last look at us. Maybe they thought they'd suddenly remember someone a little more to their liking who could do the job better than we could. If so, they were out of luck. We were the best, and they knew it.

"I understand you had some problems about a babysitter?" Uluniu looked at us in confusion and decided I was the one who must have a kid. She raised an eyebrow at me, and it went up half a centimeter higher when it was Jamin who responded.

"My son's sitter had more of a problem than I did," he said. "Somebody killed her."

"But you were ill?" asked Willem.

Jamin looked embarrassed. I said quickly, "That's all moot now; you can get a report from Ground Patrol. Meantime, we ought to get off this rock if we're going to catch up to the *Marabou* in time to do her any good.''

''You've found a new sitter, then?'' asked Uluniu, looking at Jamin this time.

Jamin looked at Willem. ''I found a retired nurse Collis seems to like. But I wish you'd look in on him after we go, Willie. Just to make sure he's okay.''

Willem nodded. ''Certainly. Certainly. Now, about the *Marabou* . . .'' From there the conversation degenerated into a rehash of last night's conversation: details of the Company's concern, the military effort that preceded us, and for variety, a few questions about the supplies I had requisitioned for the trip.

''I ordered what I thought we'd need, and I had the shuttle outfitted for a distance run. You maybe thought we wouldn't need any food or fuel?''

''What I was more concerned with,'' said Willem, ''was the laser and photar weapons, and the deflector shield—''

''Have you decided on a name for your Falcon?'' asked Francis.

Willem stared at him for interrupting. I grinned at both of them. *''Defiance.''* I hadn't actually decided on that before Pete Francis asked, but I had to come up with something if I didn't want to discuss my new weaponry. *Defiance* sounded fine, once I'd said it.

''Defiance,'' Jamin repeated, frowning at me.

''Sure, why not?''

Pete Francis grinned unexpectedly. ''Very appropriate for the Skyrider's shuttle. Shall I register it for you?''

"Sure. Yeah. Thanks," I said. "Now, can we get out of here?"

Francis looked at Willem. Nobody else had said much, and they were still staring as though Jamin, Francis, and I were some kind of bizarre aliens, but that was fine with me. I didn't feel like reassuring a bunch of VIPs who'd selected me for a job and then got uncertain about my personality.

Willem looked at them, and at me and Jamin, and reluctantly nodded. "If you're fully prepared, we won't delay you any further."

I didn't wait for anyone to confirm that. I turned around and walked. Jamin followed, a little slower, looking almost as uncertain as the VIPs. I waited till we were out of the briefing room to ask if he'd begun to have second thoughts, too. "Because if you have, I can probably get somebody else to come in your place. Should I do that?"

He glared at me. "You want more broken bones, or what?"

"You think you could break them?"

He wanted to try, I think. But for once he used some sense. "We don't have time. Let's get off this rock."

"What about Collis?"

"What about him?"

"Aren't you going to say goodbye, or anything?"

"I already did."

I couldn't interpret his expression. He still looked like he wanted to hit somebody, but maybe it wasn't me, after all. I shrugged. "Okay. Let's go."

He was silent all the way to the ready room, where

we changed into flight suits and I exchanged a few parting insults with the pilots in the rec room next door. He didn't seem to hear us. He was intent on his own thoughts, which he showed no inclination to share. The first sign he showed of any emotion other than a rather intense distaste for me was when we lifted off Home Base and I kicked out the gravity generators. I had never seen him relax before.

CHAPTER ELEVEN

The various delays we'd encountered had set us considerably behind any optimum schedule. We had to catch the *Marabou* before she fell past Earth because once inside Earth's orbit she would probably not have adequate fuel and consequent power to pull out of her dive for the sun, even with newly repaired engines. We were in a race with time and physics again. Sometimes I thought my worst enemies in the world were time and physics. Usually I was wrong.

In freefall, with Jamin beside me looking more comfortable and pleasant than I'd ever seen him before, and the controls of my beloved new *Defiance* under my hands, I dived sunward at top speed and laughed out loud at the sweet sound of those great engines. I knew no more beautiful song than that of a Falcon's engines. Unless maybe the Gypsies. . . . I could hear them singing, too.

Within minutes, Home Base dwindled in the view-screens to a speck of twinkling light far behind us, and I was dodging wild rocks and tame ones on the way to New England with my shuttle's nose toward Mars. Jamin stretched out in the seat beside me, the cold arrogance gone completely from his expression. Only the shock webbing held him to the flight seat, and that lightly. He was long and thin, and I'd thought of him as being like a plasteel spring, tense and too tightly wound. But in freefall he went almost limp, with an underlying readiness that belied the negligence of his posture. He was transformed. In even small gestures he was fluidly graceful, with the beauty of a big cat or a trained dancer in his movements.

I was about to comment on that when the Comm Link spat static at me. *"Defiance,* ah, Home Base calling the independent shuttle *Defiance.* Please respond."

I flipped a switch. *"Defiance."* The sound of that was even sweeter than the song of her engines because it meant she really was mine. But along with the thrill of belonging that I felt over that, I felt a surge of trepidation; Home Base should have no reason to call us now.

"Ah, *Defiance,* ah, this is Willem; ah, Jamin?"

He straightened, and I could see the sudden fear in his eyes. "Here, Willem. What is it? Is Collis—"

"Ah," said Willem. "Ah. Jamin. Ah." I'd never heard Willem at a loss for words before.

I knew what he was trying to say before he figured out how to say it; the intercom had been left on, and I heard something in the passenger compartment. "Damn!" I said. And yet I had more than half expected this.

"Ah," said Willem, "we can't find Collis."

If he was sick enough to vomit in freefall, he might aspirate, risking serious complications and even death before I could reach him. Fortunately, Jamin hadn't unstrapped, and I could only pray Collis had sense enough to strap himself in when we took off. I yelled something at Jamin—I don't even remember what—and slammed the gravity generators back on.

The Comm Link was still sputtering. I said, "Thanks, Willem. I think we have Collis on board." Beside me, Jamin was stunned by the sudden gravity, but at least he was alive. I hoped his son was too. But when I yelled for him, he didn't respond.

Jamin was too shaken to pilot the shuttle through those rocks; I wouldn't even trust him to go looking for Collis. And I couldn't put the *Defiance* on auto so near New England. I shouted again, and waited. There'd been no sounds since the first furtive ones I heard while Willem was stuttering over the Comm Link—a thing he was still doing, which I finally ended by cutting off the Link to Home Base.

If Collis hadn't been strapped down . . . but he'd sounded sick, and I hadn't dared leave the generators off. "Dear God," I said. Jamin looked at me, too dizzy to move and too anxious to sit still.

"Collis!" I shouted.

He sniffled. I never thought I'd be glad to hear a kid sniffle.

"Collis, are you all right?"

"I'm okay." He didn't sound okay. But he didn't sound dead, either. He sounded scared and sick and sorry; all of which was, under the circumstances, fine with me.

"Can you come forward?" I asked.

"Yes, sir."

"Do it." I glanced at Jamin, who looked grimmer and more arrogant than ever. The sudden gravity must have been hell for him, totally unprepared as he was and relaxing in freefall so gratefully after his long stay in gravity. But he wasn't about to let me see his pain.

I had my hands full while the kid was making his way to the cockpit. The wild rocks out by New England came in bunches, and even the bunches were wild. One never knew where or when to expect how many, how fast, how tightly grouped or randomly spaced; one knew only that there would be rocks, and that it would be a job to avoid them.

We were through the worst by the time the kid made his pale, shaky way into our presence. He looked as scared as he was sick, and both were justified. In full Earth gravity now, he was getting over his illness, but Jamin greeted him with hurled wrath at twenty paces that would have knocked a lesser kid down.

"What in space did you think you were doing? You might have—" He paused in mid-sentence, and I glanced at him, wondering if he suffered apoplexy.

He'd been saving all that anger since the kid first spoke over the intercom.

But it was only that he'd seen his son's face. I could see it, too, out of the corner of my eye while I dodged rocks. I stifled what would have been an imprudent grin. Collis sniffled. Jamin sighed. His anger was mostly a reaction to fear for Collis and to his own discomfort in the sudden gravity; he couldn't maintain it in the face of that angelic dismay. "Oh, Collis," he said lamely.

Collis hurtled into his arms, full of explanations and apologies, most of which I heard only parts of since they spoke into each other's shirts and hair and collars like reunited lovers.

"This is all we really needed," I said. "Just to complete the farce: a spacesick kid on our hands." When I glanced up from the controls, they were both glaring at me resentfully, like a pair of little boys caught with their hands in the cookie jar and uncertain how to maintain their dignity. I let them stew while I dodged another batch of rocks.

"It's not Collis's fault," began Jamin.

"Nobody dragged him on board, did they?" I asked.

Collis frowned at me. "It's not Papa's fault."

"It's his job to raise you right," I said. "Did he teach you to stow away when you want a ride somewhere?"

"No, but I, I mean, I," he said.

"I know." I looked at him. "So here you are. Having a nice time so far?"

Collis kept looking at me, and his eyes never wavered. "No."

"You knew you couldn't last in freefall."

"I knew the med-techs *said* I couldn't," he corrected. "I haven't been in freefall for, oh, ages, and I thought maybe . . . well . . ." He looked defensive and defiant, both at once. "I *might* have outgrown it."

"Did the med-techs say you might?"

He tried not to look at his father. "No. But I thought, I mean . . ."

Jamin hugged him. "I said he might. Someday. For space sake, Skyrider."

I dodged another flurry of rocks. "I know. So. We don't have a pharmaceutical dispenser on board. Did you bring enough medication to make the whole run in gravity?"

He really hadn't thought of that. "Why . . . no. I didn't think I'd need it."

"You mean I have to go back, after all?" asked Collis.

I shook my head. "You can't. If we take time to run you back and get you settled, we may never catch the *Marabou* in time."

"But it wouldn't take long; we're not that far out. And Papa can't—"

"You don't understand astrophysics quite well enough yet," I said. "You'll learn. Meantime, take it from me: we can't go back."

"But Papa can't—"

I looked at him and couldn't restrain the grin any longer. It wasn't kind to Jamin; he wouldn't be comfortable in gravity even with medication. But he should have thought of that. "Not to worry." I looked back at my controls. "I brought the medication.

I had a feeling we'd need it. This kid reminds me too much of somebody I used to know.''

That interested Collis. "Who, Skyrider?"

I glanced inadvertently at Jamin, and away again. "Nobody important." But I'd already said too much. I wouldn't get out of answering the question eventually, and the sooner I did, the less they might think about the answer. "Just a kid fresh out of Earth some twenty years ago." I skidded the *Defiance* sideways to miss a batch of rocks and wondered what that kid would have thought of me if she could see me now. "Her name was Melacha."

CHAPTER TWELVE

Jamin took Collis back to the passenger compartment to get him settled in. I called Company Flight
Control to let them know what had happened. To his
credit, Willem, who was still on the Comm Link,
seemed as concerned with Jamin and Collis as he was
with how the kid's presence would affect the mission.
He asked about their health before he asked whether
we'd be bringing Collis back, though he knew that if
we did, we'd have small chance of catching the
Marabou. Any other Company VIP would have asked
that first and tried to change my mind if I said we
were coming back. Willem even asked if I was sure
they'd both be okay, and did I have supplies enough
on board for three?

I had. I always stocked more than I expected to
need of most anything. I'd been caught short a time

or two, and I didn't like it. "We'll be okay, Willem,"
I said. "Don't worry." The sudden song of Gypsies
nearly drowned his reply. "Say again?"

"Jamin's medication," said Willem. "Has he
enough?"

"Oh. Yeah; I stocked that, too. Look, I'm fighting
wild rocks here; I have to go." It wasn't the rocks; it
was the Gypsies, but I wasn't going to tell him I
preferred the song of dead Gypsies to casual chatter
with him. Then he might have called us back on the
grounds that I was crazy.

As it was, he sounded almost miffed that I cut him
off, but that was his problem. I looked at the
viewscreen, humming to myself, thinking of Django.
He had been like Jamin in some ways, though the
thought hadn't occurred to me before. They didn't
look alike, but Django, like Jamin, would have been
nonplussed when I bargained with the Company for a
Falcon before I agreed to this mission. Django was a
hero. He'd have gone, like Jamin, for standard hazardous duty pay—or for nothing. He probably wouldn't
have asked about pay. He'd just have gone.

That was how it had been with the *Sunjammer*.
That was how it had always been with Django. Like
Jamin, he seemed to see things in two colors: right
and wrong. There'd been no question of his sympathies during the Colonial Incident. Not that he didn't
understand subtleties. He did. Perhaps he perceived
them more readily than most people. Like Jamin,
startled that I didn't recognize how important it was
to find a proper babysitter. They seemed to sort their

priorities before I even knew there were priorities to sort.

But Django had never been arrogant. Bewildering, self-assured, assertive, impatient, often angry, but never arrogant. Of course, maybe Jamin wasn't, either. Maybe that was just the expression he wore to conceal his pain. Because that was one way in which he and Django had been very different: Django was never ashamed of pain. He didn't call attention to it or complain when he was hurt, but he wasn't afraid to cry.

"What's that song? I don't think I've ever heard it before."

Startled, I stared up at Jamin, and for just a moment his blue eyes bore the shadows I had always seen in Django's Gypsy eyes. The hint of a smile that pulled at his lips . . .

Then I recognized the song.

"Something wrong?" asked Jamin.

I shook my head in a negative that I knew was a lie. Something had to be wrong. The Gypsies had never sung a funeral dirge to me before. Not even at Django's funeral. I started a routine systems check, trying to see everything at once.

"What's the matter with you? We've been over—"

"The Gypsies." I said it without thinking because I couldn't listen to him and concentrate on the systems checks at the same time. "That was a funeral dirge. They never sing . . ." I realized what I was saying and glanced at him.

"The Gypsies?" He looked ready to humor me. He'd heard the legend. I'd let a few people know I could hear the Gypsies before I learned to live with their songs.

"Da kine *rien*," I said. "Pay no attention." My own attention was back on the control boards, and I slipped automatically into Django's speech patterns; they were the patterns of lies. "This one thing of no importance. Usually what I do is, sometimes I sing one song while I work, that's all. Did you check the air-filter coils?"

But that, too, was a mistake. "We both checked the air filters when we . . ." he began, and paused, and when I looked at him, I knew he'd heard all the gossip. He knew how Django died. "Look, Melacha . . ."

"No, you look." I was too scared to be polite about it. "I can guess what you've heard, and I don't really care what you think. I don't have time to reason with you. There is something wrong on this shuttle, and we've got to find out what it is, and fast."

He looked dubious. "What could it be? You've just checked all the systems again. You went over the shuttle from nose to tail when you got it. What else is there?"

What else *was* there? The Gypsies kept singing. I dodged a rock and stared at the viewscreen full of stars.

"Melacha, I know how you—"

"You *don't* know," I snapped. "Shut up." What else *was* there? Had I missed something in the shuttle? Had I missed something in the supplies we carried on board? I knew I'd missed something somewhere, but what?

Jamin sat down beside me, looking fretful. At least it was a change from arrogant. I was getting tired of arrogant.

The engines were smooth and steady, just as they should be. The recycling and weapons systems checked out fine. Everything checked out fine, on the readout board. But so had it before I found the booby traps. Could I have missed one?

I'd been over every centimeter of the *Defiance*. I'd practically taken her apart and put her back together myself. If I'd missed anything in that search, it was something nobody could find. Yet I must have missed something. The Gypsies wouldn't sing a funeral dirge for fun. And besides the ship itself, there were only the supplies Jamin and I had brought on board ourselves, and Collis. He could hardly be a threat. But he was the only thing we hadn't hand-carried aboard.

Or was he? "Jamin, how did the supplies for the *Marabou* come aboard?"

"Ground Patrol brought them." He was watching me uneasily.

"Did you inspect them?"

"Ground Patrol did. And the guards you set."

"Did *you?*"

He made an impatient gesture. "No. The guards did. And Ground Patrol. What more could you ask?"

"Life, liberty, and the pursuit of happiness. Damn. Where did you put Collis?"

"In the spare passenger compartment, where else?"

"Next to the cargo hold. Damn."

He attempted an uncertain smile. "You're repeating yourself."

"I know it. Get him out of there. No, wait. You stay here." I dodged a rock absently. We were out of the worst of the flurries, and anyway, Jamin was said to be quite a good pilot. Better I should leave him to fly the *Defiance* while I cleaned house. He wouldn't find the onboard danger fast enough; he didn't really even believe there was anything to find. I knew there was. And the Gypsies might help me find it. "Take over. I'm going back there." I didn't give him time to argue. I wasn't sure we *had* time.

I should have guessed, when Jamin's medication was switched, back at Home Base. Maybe I should have guessed before that, when I first learned the *Marabou* had been sabotaged. Certainly I should have seen it all when the babysitter died and I found my Falcon full of booby traps. None of it looked like Insurrectionist activities if you really looked at it.

The *Marabou* was carrying a Company payload, so we all assumed her sabotage was an Insurrectionist act. It could conceivably have been; only the pilots and the engines were affected, and her passengers had a chance at survival. If a Belter or a Colonial were going to sabotage a liner, that's how it would be done. During the Incident, that's how it had been done, more than once.

Nobody had named the *Marabou* payload to me. I had assumed it was something important enough to justify the sabotage. But something that important would surely be shipped by military transport. What if her payload were something *un*important enough to justify the sabotage? What if neither Earth nor the Company really cared about her payload? If the *Marabou* fell all the way insystem, who would really be hurt? The Company would be out one liner's payload. Three hundred innocent civilians would die. And as a result of their deaths, the Insurrectionists would lose a lot of sympathizers.

Would anybody, even an Earther, deliberately massacre three hundred people for a political goal like that? It had seemed too far-fetched even to consider, back when the sabotage of the *Marabou* was all we knew about. But on sober reflection, it was equally ridiculous to suspect that Insurrectionists would massacre those three hundred people in order to prevent Earth from receiving a payload that hadn't even been important enough for military transport.

What Belter would switch a person's medication as a method of murder? If one had done, maybe he'd follow through by killing the little Earther babysitter, the only witness to his transgression. But she was an Earther. Transplanted with her pitiable refuse container to the alien territory of the Belt. Would she have switched the medication on request of an Insurrectionist? Her sympathies were almost certainly still with Earth and the Company.

She would have done it for Earth or for the Company. And having done, she would have been unlikely to blather about her own guilt. Surely, killing her would therefore be an unnecessary stroke. She wouldn't have suffered the guilt a Belter would for the underhanded act she had performed. She might experience some guilt; after all, she'd tried to kill a man. But from her point of view, it must have seemed as straightforward as a murder could be. Maybe hardly a murder at all: in my experience, Earthers tended to regard Belters' lives as negligible, at best.

But she must have done it, and she had been killed. Suppose Earthers sabotaged the *Marabou*. Suppose they then sent a military Falcon after her and sabotaged that, too. It would be simple enough to sabotage their own Falcon or even just to select incompetent pilots. They'd be, to all appearances, making every effort to save the poor doomed liner. And they'd be making sure their efforts failed. That way things looked blacker and blacker for the nasty Insurrectionists who were assumed to have started the whole thing.

If the Company VIPs didn't know what was going on, it would be natural for them to organize a Belter brigade—me and Jamin—to go after the liner when the military effort failed. Suppose, then, that the same Earther group who started it all wanted to stop us. First they bribed, blackmailed, or just confused poor Lunn, whose unimpeachable Belter status helped convince me the whole thing was an Insurrectionist plot. Then they hired the babysitter to switch Jamin's medication. They might have killed her afterward just because she *was* an Earther. The switch could be too easily traced to her. But anybody finding her murdered would surely look for an Insurrectionist murderer.

And killing accomplices was anyway as common among Earthers as it was uncommon among Belters. The manner of her death suggested a surprise attack by someone she trusted. In a way, she must have been as much a used and discarded pawn as the civilians on the *Marabou*. And I'd bought it. I'd bought it all. I tracked the switch to the babysitter and found her dead, and just as I was supposed to do, I blamed unknown Insurrectionists. And set an Earther guard on my Falcon.

Now, with the Gypsies singing a funeral dirge and the bitter surmise adding up to a very ugly picture, I might have kicked myself for general stupidity if I hadn't been so busy trying to stay alive.

CHAPTER THIRTEEN

On my way to the hold I paused in the living quarters only long enough to pluck Collis out of his new residence and push him toward the cockpit. "Get up front with your father. Close the air lock behind you."

Startled into obedience, he was out of his quarters before he stopped to ask, "What's wrong? If I close the air lock, won't that—"

"Do it." I gave him a little shove and tried not to notice the brave white look he gave me. He went. I waited till he grasped the air lock handle, and gave him an encouraging smile when he hesitated. Reluctantly, he swung it shut.

Fighting my own panic now, I dived into the cargo hold and slammed the lock between it and the living quarters. That put two inner locks between the cockpit and whatever gift the Earthers had bestowed upon us. Jamin and Collis would have a chance even if I failed.

Sometimes Gypsy songs had words. This one hadn't. Not even in Romani, which I wouldn't have understood but would have recognized. There was only the music, melancholy and mysterious, tugging at my mind. My heart pounded a frantic rhythm out of time with the song.

The *Marabou*'s supplementary foodstuffs were in the crate nearest me. It bore a Company seal. I banged my knuckles on it and bent one of the Company's cheap pry bars getting it open. Packets of emergency rations, sealed in bright red plastic that glittered in the cold glare of the hold's overhead lights tumbled onto the deck as I delved in among them, searching for something that didn't belong.

The Gypsies kept singing.

I kicked aside crackling bright parcels of foodstuffs and deserted that crate for the other, which was supposed to contain engine parts and tools for use on the liner. That crate, too, bore the Company seal, indicating that it, like the other, had been carefully examined by Company personnel before it was sealed, then closely guarded until it was safely aboard the *Defiance*. But I didn't even have to touch the crate to know. The Gypsy song faded as I approached it. In the unexpected silence I could hear the roar of blood in my ears, much louder than the steady background thrum of the engines.

There was an intercom on the bulkhead next to the crate. I flipped it on while I took up another pry bar.

"It wasn't in the foodstuffs." I hooked the bar under the latch and leaned against it. "I'm opening the other crate now. If I find—" I stumbled when the latch broke, and banged my knuckles again. "Damn."

Jamin said, "Skyrider?"

"Hang on." Very carefully I lifted the top off the crate. "It's here." I closed my eyes, resting my unsteady hands on the edge of the crate. "Collis, did you close the air lock like I told you to?" My knees were unsteady, too.

"It's closed." Jamin's voice, near and familiar; the wonders of modern technology. "What have you found?"

I opened my eyes reluctantly. "A little souvenir from our friends, whoever they are." It was neat, small, and deadly. They'd made no effort to disguise it as part of the equipment; I should have had no reason to open that crate. Not after Ground Patrol and the Company guards inspected it. "I'm going to try to space it. There's not much time."

"Be careful." Jamin's voice was sharp. "It may be rigged against tampering."

"Not much I can do about that." I found a small crate nearby and wrestled its top off. The contents, mostly spare hand tools, I dumped unceremoniously on the deck. "How clean does our flight path look?" I asked absently.

"You know it's clean." Now he was impatient, puzzled. "Except for a few wild rocks, there's nothing within a hundred kilometers of us. What's going on back there?"

Righting the small crate again, I set it next to the

equipment crate. "Collis has a lot of stories about what a hotshot pilot you were during the Incident." The small crate looked about the right relative size. "Think you could pilot a holed Falcon?" I took a bottle of sealant off the rack.

"If I had to," said Jamin.

Good old arrogant, self-confident Jamin. I almost grinned, imagining his expression. "And could you dead-dock it with a liner?" I inverted the bottle and blinked against the pungent reek of sealant foam spraying out.

Jamin didn't hesitate. He was arrogant, but he wasn't an idiot. "I don't know. I've never tried." He paused, and I listened to the hiss and sputter of sealant and tried not to breathe. "Don't be a hero, Skyrider. What the hell is going on? What are you doing?"

"I'm no hero. I'm a realist. I can't pilot a liner. Can you dead-dock?"

"I can try."

"That's good enough." The nozzle tried to jump out of my hands, spattering dark blobs of sealant on the deck. I turned my face away to take a deep breath and held the bottle steady. "What I've got back here is one hell of a dirty trick, and probably not much time. It looks like whoever planted this thing wanted to watch the fireworks. He's probably got a telescope on us from Home Base. But I guess he didn't think I'd open this crate, or he didn't know I'm manic about sealant." One cannister was standard equipment for a peacetime shuttle. The workers had sneered at me when I had all the extra racks installed. They should be here now. "We have a chance, anyway."

My sealant bottle was empty. The thick, gray, viscous stuff had sprayed out in a heavy foam that would adhere to nearly anything it touched and quickly harden in place. Ordinarily it was used to patch holed bulkheads before air pressure from inside could tear the holes larger. What I hoped it would do now was prevent a holed bulkhead.

The bottom and sides of the small crate were unevenly coated. I dropped the empty bottle and turned back to the equipment crate. "If I blow it," I said, "you'll have a fine mess on your hands. And I'll lay you odds our friends will come after you personally. So don't forget the weapons I had installed. And take good care of the *Defiance* for me, will you?"

"You get back up here and take good care of her yourself."

"Sure. In a minute." Moving as quickly as I dared, I lifted the deadly little device out of the equipment crate and dropped it into the sealant-coated smaller crate, then grabbed another bottle and sprayed more sealant on top of it. I didn't know how much time I had. The sealant would cushion the bomb against shocks, as well as muffling the explosion if it blew before I got it spaced. But maybe if I'd tried to space the thing naked I could have got it out before it blew. I didn't know, and I could seal it faster than I could space it. Too late for second guesses now.

The sealant was already nearly solid, forming a sturdy closed nest for the bomb. Grabbing up the little crate full of death, I headed for the outside disposal chute. And there again we'd been lucky; if this thing had been in the living quarters, I'd have been in trouble. Every disposal chute there led directly to the shuttle's recycling unit. But in cargo holds there was always one chute that functioned as a miniature air lock through which one could dump dangerous or offensive materials directly into space.

What I had was both dangerous and offensive. My hands were shaking again. I had a hard time getting the inner chute door open. And a harder time stuffing the sealant-filled crate inside.

"Skyrider? What's happening?"

I slammed the inner door shut too hard when I finally got the crate through it. It jammed. "Be with you in a minute." Pulling the door open, I wasted precious seconds determining that nothing was wrong with the closing mechanism; the malfunction had been due to human panic. I closed it again, more gently this time. It caught.

"Skyrider?"

"Listen, I really don't have time to chat." With one hand I grabbed up another bottle of sealant while with the other I manipulated the sequence of controls necessary to activate the outside chute door.

"If you don't tell me what's happening pretty damn soon," said Jamin, "I'm coming back there to see for myself."

Since I'd done everything there was to be done, and could now only wait to see whether it had been enough, I would gladly have chatted with Jamin to his heart's content, if I'd been able to think of anything to say. All I could think about was how damn slow I'd been at getting that thing sealed and into the chute—and whether I'd been too slow.

The controls blinked. The inner door was locked, the outer beginning to open. I held the sealant bottle ready in sweat-slippery hands. The sharp odor of the two full bottles I'd already used burned my eyes and nose. The lock couldn't be hurried. The computer was taking its own sweet time getting the outer door open, and I couldn't even watch the process. The computer would signal when the door was open and the contents ejected. My subjective time sense was shot to hell. I didn't know whether I'd been waiting seconds, minutes, or even hours.

I'd just begun to think I'd made it when the world blew up.

CHAPTER FOURTEEN

It felt and sounded like the whole world had blown up. When I could see again, it looked like it, too. But since I was still there to see it, of course it had only been a small part of the world that exploded.

The sealant around the bomb helped absorb some of its force, and a lot of the blast took the path of least resistance, out into space through the opening chute door. But it was a small opening for a big explosion.

The inner door was never meant to withstand excess pressure from outside. It stayed in one piece, which I later found on the far side of the hold. At the time, I wasn't paying a lot of attention to what was in how many pieces where. I wasn't quite sure I was all in one piece: at the moment of the blast, something slammed against me and banged me solidly against the bulkhead, away from the damaged chute.

That probably saved my life. I might otherwise have found myself forced by air pressure through the chute, along with a large part of the hold's atmosphere and everything else that wasn't fastened down. Since the chute, even torn apart by an explosion, was considerably smaller in circumference than I was, that was an even less attractive thought than just getting spaced in an ordinary way.

But I wasn't thinking about that, either. All I could think of was that I'd dropped my bottle of sealant and I was losing air pressure fast. My head hurt. *"Django!"* I'm not sure whether I really called his name aloud. I tried to. I was back in another shuttle and another time, scrambling for the sealant I'd dropped, forgetting there were several more bottles in their racks nearby.

Ice crystals formed a brief glittering fog while I scrambled across the deck on all fours, groping for the sealant. Emergency generators hummed to life, increasing the general chaos in their automatic effort to retain the precious atmosphere by moving it forcibly away from the holed bulkhead. That gave me a few extra seconds in which to breathe, and I used them.

When I got the bottle picked up again, I couldn't seem to hold it. I got it inverted all right, but the nozzle slid out of my hands and I had to lean against the bulkhead to keep from falling. The Gypsies were singing. I was distantly aware of someone shouting my name. I ignored it.

With great care and precision I balanced the bottle of sealant under my arm and got the nozzle into my working hand. I didn't even wonder why the other one didn't work. That was far less important than patching the bulkhead. I knew that much and was proud of myself for remembering it. But I'd forgot just why it was so important. Perhaps the point was to stop the awful howling of the wind so I could hear the Gypsies sing.

They weren't singing a funeral dirge this time. I couldn't quite identify the song. There was a curious star-sparkled darkness before my eyes. The ominous scream of escaping atmosphere decreased till it was only a whine, then silence. Sealant hissed quietly out of my bottle, covering and recovering the damaged chute, and the emergency generators changed their tone as the computer recognized the success of my efforts and started pumping fresh atmosphere into the chamber.

But I was still intent on patching that hole. Dull-witted with shock and terror, I dropped the empty sealant bottle and stared wildly around till I found another, grabbed it, inverted it, and with patient stupidity began to build on my patch job, mounding the blessed gray gunk where the chute had been. My eyes streamed with tears from the reek of it, and my aim wasn't perfect. By the time the second bottle was empty, it wasn't very good at all. Still, I reached for a third bottle, and I would have used it if I'd had the strength to lift it.

I hadn't. And I could still hear the awful roar of that wind. It took a long while to realize the sound was only in my mind. My head hurt. I tried to put a hand on it, but my arm wouldn't work right. The hold lights seemed brighter than I remembered; I saw the wreckage around me with a terrible, angry clarity. Sealant was splattered everywhere, some of it mixed with packing material, bits of metal and plastic, and even air-filter material. Someone was shouting at me. But Django wasn't there.

For some reason I never did drop that last sealant bottle. Clinging to it with fond determination, I studied the hold for a while and then peered curiously down at my arm that didn't work. There was a spreading stain of red on the shoulder of my flight suit. "How untidy," I said in surprise.

"What? Skyrider, what are you talking about? What's going on?"

Puzzled, I looked around blankly and didn't see anyone. How odd, I thought, to be questioned by a voice from nowhere. I always flew alone since Django died. And I didn't remember taking out a passenger shuttle. Had the Gypsies finally decided to speak to me? They wouldn't if I wasn't dead. I didn't feel dead. I glared around again, suspiciously. "Who's that?" My voice sounded high and thin and small, like the voice of a frightened child.

"Me. Jamin. Who did you think?"

Jamin? I remembered a sardonic grin, arrogant eyes. "Oh. Jamin." I smiled with deep satisfaction at my verbal acumen. "Hi. Are you still here?"

"Where would I go? Will you tell me what's happening? What are you doing?"

The starred darkness swirled bright and silent before my eyes. "Oh, I'm just sitting here, I guess."

"Sitting there? Sitting? What do you mean? Sitting where? Why? What's going on?"

"I don't know." Bother. And I'd been feeling so clever, recognizing his voice that way. I peered at my feet stretched out straight in front of me. Why *was* I sitting there? I vaguely remembered leaning against the bulkhead for some reason, but I certainly didn't remember sitting down. Yet there I was, with my back to the bulkhead and a bottle of sealant in my lap. "I guess I got tired."

"You got tired." There was something odd about his tone, but I couldn't tell what it meant.

"Yeah. I got tired." I sighed. If he were as clever as I, I wouldn't have to repeat myself like this.

"Skyrider?"

Startled, I opened my eyes and blearily surveyed my surroundings. "You know, this hold's a terrible mess. Sealant all over. Somebody should tidy up in here." I thought about that. "Sealant smells bad; did you ever notice that?"

"I've noticed."

"But I guess I patched the bulkhead."

"You guess you patched the bulkhead." He sounded incredulous.

"What's so strange about that?" Curious, I peered dizzily at the bulging mass of sealant over the damaged chute. I even considered going over to it, to see if maybe it needed a little more work anywhere, but when I tried to get up, I fell over.

"I'm coming back there," said Jamin.

I levered myself upright again, sitting straight and alert against the bulkhead, practicing breathing. I was

179

getting good at it, I thought. "I don't think you can. The atmosphere is kind of thin just now. Probably the air lock won't open yet." I admired the dancing red stars. "It's cold, too."

"Skyrider."

I looked through pinwheeled darkness at the bulging mass where the outside chute had been. "But I did patch it. So everything must be all right."

He didn't answer that right away. When he did, it seemed to me his tone was odd again, but I still couldn't tell why. "Everything must be all right."

"Why do you keep repeating what I say?" I asked plaintively.

"Skyrider." He waited a moment, and when I didn't say anything, he asked patiently, "Are you all right?"

I nodded earnestly, remembered he couldn't see me, and said cheerfully, "Sure. No problem. I'm fine. How 'bout you?"

His answer, if any, was lost among the gathering stars.

CHAPTER FIFTEEN

When I woke, there was an anxious cherub watching me. I managed a frayed, uncertain smile at him. His answering grin transformed him into the mischievous boy I knew. "Hi, Collis." My voice sounded weak, even to me.

"Papa says you shouldn't talk." He put out a hand to stop me from sitting up. "And you're s'posed to lie still. You lost a lot of blood, you know."

"Did I?" I let him push me back against the pillows. I was in my own bunk, with a neat immobilizing bandage on my injured shoulder. "How'd I get in here?"

He looked smug. "Papa brought you."

"In gravity? How?"

"He carried you. He's strong, even in gravity."

The lies that man told his son! Strong, even in

181

gravity, was he? If he really carried me all the way from the cargo hold, he was a fine one to berate me for macho displays. "Is he all right?"

Collis looked surprised. "Sure. He's okay. Why wouldn't he be? You were the one that got exploded at."

"He shouldn't have . . ." But the look in the kid's eyes stopped me. It was none of my business what Jamin told his son. "Never mind. How long—" The *Defiance* lurched so hard and suddenly that Collis had to grab a freefall handhold to keep from being hurled to the deck. I reacted without thinking. Leaping out of my bunk, I thrust Collis in it and punched the intercom button, then grabbed a handhold of my own as dizziness swirled bright stars across my field of vision. "Strap down," I told the kid as the *Defiance* lurched again. "Jamin, what in space are you doing?"

"Stay in bed. Everything's under control." He sounded as self-assured as ever, but it was my shuttle he was throwing around.

"What's under control?" We lurched again and I braced myself, watching Collis buckle in. "You call that control? What's going on?"

"There's a Colonial fighter chasing us. I'll handle it."

"The hell you will. This is my shuttle." I told Collis, "Stay put for now, okay?"

"What?" asked Jamin.

"I said try to keep us alive till I get there." I didn't wait for his answer. With a quick grin to reassure Collis, I released my grip on the handhold under the intercom and prayed Jamin could hold the ship steady; I wasn't any too steady myself just then.

I made it to the cockpit with only one bad moment, when the *Defiance* lurched just as I let go a handhold. I stumbled, crashed against the bulkhead with my bandaged shoulder, and had to wait a long moment for my vision to clear before I could go on.

Jamin greeted me with a scowl. "You're white as a miner. Get back to bed. You're no use here; hell, you can't even stand up. You're not fit to fly."

"Usually I fly sitting down."

"For gods' sake."

"That, too." I made it to the pilot's seat without incident and carefully lowered myself into it. Jamin had, with unexpected tact, remained in the auxiliary control seat even while alone in the cockpit. It didn't make any real difference; the shuttle could be flown as well from either seat. But the pilot's seat was mine.

I looked at the readouts and then at Jamin. If the Colonial warrior had been firing on us, Jamin had been doing some fancy flying; we hadn't taken a hit. "What have you got on our tail?"

He looked oddly defensive, like a child denied expected praise. "I didn't get it on our tail. It got there by itself." He flipped the aft screen to show me the Starbird, just as it fired on us again.

His reaction was as quick as anyone could ask. Quicker than mine just then, when pain and fatigue dulled my mind. He sent the *Defiance* spinning so neatly out of the line of fire, it seemed almost as though he had anticipated the little Starbird's move. I watched it spin off the screen. Starbirds were the Patrol's deadliest fighters. I'd never heard of one being sold out of Earth's military service, but a number of them had been commandeered by Insurrectionists during the Incident, and this one bore the unmistakable bright blazon of the vanquished Colonial Fleet on its wings.

Jamin armed our weapons while I watched the Starbird circle back into range. "I had those installed for Patrol boats," I said, "not for Colonial warriors."

He stared in exasperation. "He's firing on us. We're in a Falcon, in case you forgot. Not a Starbird. And we're throwing power into internal gravity. How long do you think we can outmaneuver a hostile Starbird without firing back?"

"Not long. We don't need long. And I didn't say we wouldn't fire. I just don't want to hurt anyone. Relinquish controls."

He didn't want to. But he did it. The Starbird had got an angle on us, and I slid the *Defiance* smoothly out of the line of fire. She handled beautifully, a revelation after the worn-out wallowing tubs I'd been flying for the Company. She was as responsive as if she were an extension of my body. If I hadn't been in love with her before, I'd have fallen in love while we danced our elusive ballet with that Starbird. Under my delighted control she could do cartwheels so gracefully that a passenger balanced on his head wouldn't have fallen. Jamin had flown her well, but he didn't have the feel for her that I had; he wasn't in love with her.

We caught the Starbird in the laser screen and with

infinite caution and perfect coordination fired a single volley across the Starbird's bright tail. At the same time I punched the Colonial combination into the Comm Link, hoping it hadn't been changed since the Incident. "That was a warning, Starbird. We're on a rescue mission. Do you read?"

In answer, he threw another burst of fire at us, and my sweet *Defiance* skittered daintily sideways almost before I asked her to. Flying a shuttle like this wasn't a conscious process. It was like walking or breathing or fighting: I didn't have to think out each step of the process. As soon as I knew what had to be done, we did it. Just like that.

Now I was angling for position on the Starbird, and talking while I did it, in an effort to keep the Colonial pilot's mind off my movements. "I don't know who you are, but you've got your priorities on sideways." The Starbird was beautiful, her moves as graceful as my Falcon's, and she was enough smaller to have an edge on us in a protracted battle. But I didn't intend to engage in a protracted battle. Her pilot was good, but he was out of practice. Not enough rock dodging lately. I could see it in the way the bird slid wide when she spun; the same mistake Jamin had made. "Do you read me, Starbird? We are on a rescue mission. We are not a military target."

"I read you, Earther." He fired again. And missed again.

I ignored the verbal slur. His voice had sounded vaguely familiar, but I ignored that, too. "The important part of the *Marabou*'s payload is three hundred civilian lives," I said. "If we can space her cargo, we probably will. But not her passengers."

"What's the *Marabou* to do with you?" His tone was incredulous.

"We're trying to save her, that's all." I had to spin away from another laser blast.

"Very funny, Earther." Where had I heard that voice before? I couldn't place it and hadn't time to dwell on it.

"Listen, rock head, because I'll only say this once: I am not an Earther. We are not a military target. Neither is the *Marabou*. Not with three hundred civilians aboard. I don't know what you've been told about her or us, but those civilians deserve a chance to live, and we're trying to provide it. So go home. And tell your organizers to think first, next time. In case it hasn't occurred to you, it's bad form to kill noncombatants. Especially when we're not at war." I had been moving all the time I was talking, and so had he, but I'd been supplying Rat Johnson for years, and consequently running that gauntlet of wild rocks till delicate shuttle maneuvering had become automatic, even in the Company's awkward tubs. In the *Defiance* I felt invincible.

The Starbird's pilot wasn't so slow that I'd say he had to think things through before he could move, but he wasn't working with his ship; he was fighting her. I got the angle I wanted. He didn't.

I really didn't want to hurt him. That was why I had to be so careful of the angle before I fired. All I could reasonably hope for was one such chance, but one was all I needed. When I was sure of it, I fired a blast that went straight across his nose, just close enough to blind him and maybe singe that pretty paint job. "Go home, Starbird. You're out of your league."

It worked. An inarticulate growl was his only audible response. The Starbird stayed where it was; he couldn't take a chance on moving till he could see again, unless he was even crazier than I was. I hoped he wasn't.

"Bye-bye, birdie." I grinned as I flipped the *Defiance* over, out of the line of the Starbird's last blind shot at us.

His response to my cheerful leave-taking was articulate enough, but unprintable.

I'd left the intercom on, so Collis knew what was happening. I asked him if he was still strapped in.

"Yes." His voice was small, but steady.

"Then hang on." I hit the thrusters, and we watched the Colonial Starbird dwindle to a speck of bright in the aft viewscreens. By the time her pilot could see again, we'd be so far out of range he'd never pick us up. The *Defiance* had come through her first firefight without a scorch.

And we had one more piece to the puzzle. That pilot obviously didn't believe we were on a rescue mission. But he was out there waiting for us when we came by. Somebody had been feeding the Colonials some kind of lies. Probably the same somebody who had sabotaged the *Marabou,* the military rescue mission, and us. Before we met that Starbird, I had begun to wonder whether my reasoning that led to the conclusion that Earthers were behind the whole thing was maybe a trifle paranoid.

Now I was convinced it wasn't. And there wasn't the smallest remaining question in my mind as to whether I'd choose sides this time if Earth and the Colonies declared war again. I'd already chosen sides.

And the way I felt, I figured if nobody else got that war started, I might just have to do it myself. The *Defiance* didn't have a whole lot of firepower, but if I found out who exactly planned this brutal charade, I'd use what I had. In a pinch, if I couldn't find the culprits, I might try to level Earth's VIP City. That should get the guilty party, and the solar system might just smell a little cleaner afterward.

CHAPTER SIXTEEN

Maybe that Starbird pilot took home the message I gave him. At any rate, we had no further trouble with Colonials. Nobody chased us; nobody lurked in ambush; and no new surprises turned up on board the *Defiance*. We might have been alone in the universe for all we saw or heard of its other inhabitants.

That should have been comforting, and maybe it was to Jamin and Collis. But not to me. The absence of obstructions set my nerves on edge. No Patrol, no Colonials, no wild rocks, no nothing . . . and we were sticking to our filed flight plan. It had been years since I'd filed a plan and then actually flown it. Longer still since I'd flown far enough out of the Belt to be free of wild rocks. Not that they were exactly thick, except in patches, in the Belt; but they were there. And the Patrol was always a hazard on my flights. But not on this one.

I hadn't realized how accustomed I was to treading the taut edge of Death till I stepped off, onto this safe journey, where nothing I was doing was illegal and nowhere I was going would be dangerous till we caught up with the *Marabou*. Nor would I have believed, if anyone had told me in advance of it, that to take such a safely approved journey would feel so unnervingly *wrong*. In a way, it was as bad as the unchambered atmosphere of Earth; unnatural. I didn't like it.

I was uncomfortable in my relationship with Jamin and Collis, too, for exactly the same contradictory reasons. It was too comfortable. We fell into a natural routine very like the daily routine I would imagine for a nuclear family. I'd never really known family life, and on some level I must have thought I was missing something pretty special. But when I got it, I didn't know what to do with it.

Once safely out of the Belt, we could leave the computer in charge of the *Defiance* most of the time, leaving us free to eat, sleep, work, and play together. The very steadiness and security of that troubled me. Outwardly, I was enjoying myself and my new little family, but inside I felt lost and a little scared.

In the "mornings," Collis and I, who were both early risers, programmed the dispenser for breakfast and took turns selecting from the computer's reading material. Thus armed, we entered Jamin's chamber with a tray and read to him while he ate. Afterward Collis cleared the breakfast things while Jamin got himself up and I ran routine systems checks in the cockpit. Collis usually joined me later for what we called his piloting lessons. Young as he was, he was a quick study in the cockpit and seemed to have a natural feel for the Falcon's eccentricities and abilities. He also became very good at Planets, beating me one game out of three; he had a perfect poker face and suckered me more than once with those wide innocent eyes.

I wouldn't have admitted it out loud, but of course I had fallen in love with Collis the first time I met him. I enjoyed our morning sessions, during which I interspersed the usual lessons on computer programming and quantum physics with impromptu lectures on the best methods for evading Patrol boats and concealing contraband. Since Jamin rested for an hour or two after breakfast, Collis and I were assured of that much time alone together; and though I felt a bit awkward when I realized he had begun to look upon me as a second parent, I was happy in the relationship as long as nobody was looking.

Jamin, however, couldn't be depended upon not to look, as I discovered to my embarrassment one morning when he came in half an hour earlier than usual and caught me hugging Collis in an excess of pride and delight over his mastery of a particularly difficult "fight or flight" plan I'd programmed into the simulator.

If I'd had any time to think about it, I might have reacted differently. But Jamin's arrival caught me completely by surprise. I had been reserved with Collis whenever I knew Jamin was watching, and

Collis seemed to accept that as unquestioningly as he accepted the shuttle's eccentricities, or Jamin's. The things he loved were eccentric. I suppose, in moments alone, he must have wondered why we were eccentric in just the ways we were, and perhaps he formulated theories to explain us. He'd have needed quite a theory to explain me.

Jamin's opening remark was innocuous enough. "Hi, guys," he said, and I dropped Collis as convulsively as if I'd been caught in an illicit love affair.

In a way, of course, I had. God forbid anyone should notice I loved the kid. "What the hell are you doing here?"

Jamin looked surprised and puzzled. "Where else would I be?"

"I don't know. Napping or something. Whatever you usually do with your mornings."

Collis looked at the chronometer. "You usually come half an hour later, Papa."

Jamin looked at him. "I didn't know I'd be unwelcome."

I stood up. "You're not. In fact, you're more than welcome. It's about time you showed up. I'm sick of spending every morning babysitting. You can take over, and for once I can have a little time to myself before lunch."

They both just stared at me as I left the cockpit. I didn't have to turn around to see them. I could feel their matching blue eyes, wide with startled hurt, watching my back.

The worst of it was that I wasn't sick of babysitting, and I didn't want time to myself. I wanted to be with the two of them, with my happy little family unit. When Collis had first begun to share with me his daily trials and triumphs, I'd been alarmed and awkward, and tried to avoid his attentions. But he wouldn't let me, and after a while I didn't try anymore. Except when Jamin was looking.

Nor had Jamin turned out to be the unlikable, arrogant rock jockey I had originally considered him. The more familiar I became with his mannerisms and facial expressions, the more I realized he was, secretly, as unsure of himself as most of the people I knew, and pleasanter really, than most. Certainly pleasanter than I.

He was always in pain, but he never complained. The times he suffered most were discernible only because he became more arrogant then; it was his unconscious defense against weakness, the only concession he made.

In his own environment he could have been as tough as any Belter, but in gravity, however stubbornly he might try to conceal it, he was fragile. So fragile that I was almost afraid to touch him, as though I thought he might break. But he wouldn't break.

He had a way of looking at me when something happened to remind us both of his limitations. A look that dared me to speak of it and at the same time pleaded for silence. . . . It would take a hell of a lot to break a man like that. I saw him once trying to shift a box of cargo to get at an inspection plate behind it. Collis could have moved that box with ease. Jamin sidled it along the deck till it caught on a

193

protruding bolt, and that was it. The thing weighed maybe ten pounds Standard, and he couldn't lift it. I let him know I was there when I saw him trying to wedge his toe under it in an effort to get it past that bolt. And he gave me that look. Defiant, poignant, fierce. . . .

I didn't say anything. I just moved the box for him and left the hold in silence.

No freefall mutant could endure Earth gravity indefinitely. That Jamin tried to, for the sake of his son, was impressive. That he had managed to maintain his composure and keep his secret as long as he had was almost incredible. Collis had no idea how inherently fragile his father was in gravity. And Jamin wouldn't tell him. Perhaps he couldn't.

Pride can do that: it can make a man, or break him. It can kill him. Or it can just leave him isolated, as I had just isolated myself by my defiant pride that would not permit me to admit my love for a boy . . . or for his father.

I was, after all, the great Skyrider: risk taker, lawbreaker; death defier; outlaw queen. . . . Hotshot Skyrider, the loner who didn't need anybody's love. That was me.

Sure. That was me. The woman who could hear dead Gypsies. The pilot who could save the *Marabou*. The smuggler who could catch and match Rat Johnson's rock with no synch system and outrun the Patrol in a crippled ship.

I could lie on my bunk all day and think up stirring labels for what I was. But it wouldn't change the fact that I was also the surrogate mother of Collis and the so-called friend of his father. Walking out on them in a fit of adolescent pique wouldn't change that, either. Somehow, I was going to have to reconcile my self-image with reality.

"Oh, space it." I sat up abruptly, and made a face at the dull reflection of my movement in the polished plasteel bulkhead. "Psych-tender jargon. Keep it up, Skyrider. Maybe you can work your way into a real state of crazy."

My voice sounded hollow in the empty room. I shut up. And got up. It was our custom for Jamin to program lunches, but I never liked to get too stuck on customs. A person should remain flexible, open to change. Besides, I was hungry, and Jamin never prepared lunch that early in the day.

I never was much of a cook. Fortunately, with the dispenser, one didn't have to be. At the start of the trip I had fed into it all the recipe programs I had collected over the years, from Gypsies and miners and settlers, Earthers and Belters, books and magazines, and even an occasional old-fashioned chef. All I had to do was punch up the combination for the recipe I wanted, and the dispenser did the rest.

Before the trip I had stocked the contraband compartment with a case of genuine Earther beer that I'd brought back from my trip there and with a jug of real fruit juice my mother had given me. Both were worth their weight in malite on Home Base, so I hadn't liked to leave them unprotected in my quarters there. And neither would be worth much at all in Earth orbit, so we might just as well drink them before we got there. I programmed lunch and got the drinks out of the hold while the dispenser was contemplating my instructions.

When Jamin and Collis showed up in the galley to prepare lunch, I was ready for them. I had the table set, the meal laid out, and drinks poured. They paused in the doorway, looking at me and the elaborate meal I had prepared. Neither of them made any reference, then or later, to the scene in the cockpit. Jamin didn't say anything at first; he just looked at me. Collis gestured toward the table and said, "What's that?"

"Lunch," I said.

He made a face at me, his eyes smiling. "I meant in our glasses."

"Fruit juice, in yours."

"Real fruit?"

"Genuine, all the way from Earth."

"Wow." He sat at his place and touched his glass but didn't lift it. "What's in yours and Papa's?"

"Beer."

Jamin lifted an eyebrow. "Real beer?"

"Genuine, all the way from Earth."

"Wow." He hesitated a moment longer, then went to his place at the table and sat. Like Collis, he touched his glass but didn't lift it. "How'd you manage that?"

I took the remaining seat and refrained from touching my glass. "I managed. Go ahead and try it."

They both hesitated, still touching their glasses, and I started trying to formulate apologies for the way I had acted earlier. Then Collis lifted his glass, looked at his father, looked at me, and said, "I think we should, I mean, is it all right to make a toast with a drink that doesn't have, um, what makes you drunk in it?''

"Alcohol," said Jamin.

"I think so," I said.

"Then I'd like to make a toast."

I don't know whether they'd planned it or whether Jamin just guessed what was coming. He didn't say anything. He just took up his glass of beer and waited for Collis to make his toast.

"To the Skyrider," said Collis.

"Um," I said.

"To the Skyrider," said Jamin.

"I—" I said.

"You're supposed to pick up your glass, and then we bump them all together," said Collis. "That makes it a real toast."

"Oh," I said.

Jamin held his glass toward mine.

"Why?" I said.

"Because that's how it's done," Collis explained patiently.

"I meant," I said.

"Hush, Melacha," said Jamin.

"Oh." I looked at him. Those clear blue eyes were laughing at me. As usual. "Oh." I picked up my glass, and we bumped them all together, then drank.

It was a very good lunch.

CHAPTER SEVENTEEN

Jamin was weakening visibly with each day that passed. With no opportunity to spend even a part of his time in freefall, he simply could not survive in the same environment as his son. Nor could Collis survive even a short while in the environment required by his father; in desperation, and quite against Jamin's wishes, we tried it. We could lessen the gravity very little before Collis showed signs of illness. Long before the gravity was low enough to give Jamin any real relief, Collis was violently sick.

With that much gravity, it wouldn't have been the hazard it was in freefall, but it was a hazard because it didn't end. He begged me to keep on with the experiment. No matter how Jamin tried to hide his discomfort, he could not conceal his pallor, or the bruised look of the flesh around his eyes, or his decreasing ability to perform even the lightest of shipboard maintenance duties. For the first time, Collis had become aware of how severe the problem really was.

But our efforts were useless. Collis could not stop vomiting, and Jamin could not relax. If I lowered the gravity enough to give Jamin any relief, Collis got sicker, and the danger of aspiration increased. For a while they were both frail and worn and so damnably brave I could have kicked them. It did nobody any good. I called off the experiments.

They had already tried all the med-techs' drugs and treatments for motion- and spacesickness with no success. And on the *Defiance* they both tried just to tough it out, in their separate ways, with an equal lack of success.

I kept remembering Collis's assertion that if there were medicines to keep his father well in gravity, there must be something to keep Collis well in freefall. Of course, Jamin wasn't exactly well in gravity. That was beside the point. There was medication to ease the strain, to keep him going, to keep him alive for a while. There damn well ought, I thought, to be something to do that for Collis in freefall.

I became obsessed with the idea, as who wouldn't who had to live in close quarters with two heroes who could not survive each other's natural environment and nonetheless were determined to do so? In a frenzy of helpless frustration, one afternoon I tapped the computer for all the information it had on the subjects of Fallers in gravity and spacesick Grounders. It wasn't any help at all. My father had pioneered the study of medication to keep Fallers alive in gravity, and I knew more about that than there was in the standard library package programmed into my computer. And I'd learned more during the experiments Collis and I conducted than there was on file about Grounders who suffered spacesickness.

But I was damn well going to find a med-tech in Earth orbit who knew more than my computer and I, and who could help Collis. Because if his inner ear problem, whatever it was, could be mended, then he could endure a life in freefall with much less immediate distress and long-term damage than Jamin suffered in gravity.

The Company could pay for it. If we survived this mission, they'd owe Jamin a hell of a lot more than that. By the time we came in Comm range of the *Marabou,* I'd begun to work out exactly how I would convince the Company of their obligation. Jamin had been a fool to settle for nothing more than hazardous duty pay. But I was an old hand at extortion, and if we docked safely with the *Marabou,* we'd be in a perfect position for it. Those three hundred passengers would make fine hostages. Maybe I could even get the Company to pay for the weapons I'd had installed on the *Defiance.* The biggest problem I could foresee was how I would keep Jamin from spoiling the show by openly admitting willingness to bring in the *Marabou* whether or not the Company agreed to my demands.

First, though, my biggest problem would be to dock safely with the *Marabou.* When we got their engineer on the Comm Link, I asked straightaway whether they had been able to determine what damage, if any, the military rescue effort had done to the docking facilities.

They couldn't tell.

"Did you even look?" I asked.

The disembodied voice that had sounded so glad to hear us sounded less glad then. "We haven't had time."

"You haven't had time! What were you doing, playing Planets?"

"With both engines and half the computer systems down, we've spent most of our time cannibalizing one engine to mend the other. What spare time we have, we use for sleeping . . . and for trying to keep the passengers halfway calm."

"Well, how far have you got?"

"With the passengers? We put the most mutinous in Sick Bay, under heavy sedation. The rest are only hysterical."

"I meant with the engines."

"We've done what we can. If you brought the equipment and parts we asked for, we may yet make it. That's assuming you also brought a pilot who knows how to manhandle a crippled monster."

"She shouldn't be crippled when you've finished, surely?"

"She sure as hell won't be a virgin."

I ignored the confusingly mixed metaphor; the engineer was under a strain. "Jamin can fly her. But how are your gravity generators?"

"In good condition. Thank the gods. If we had to

deal with these panicky dirt dwellers in freefall, I don't know what would have happened."

"But you can turn the gravity off?"

"Why the hell would we?"

Jamin was sitting next to me, his bruised eyes closed, his body slumped, his breathing painfully audible. All I could think about was getting him into freefall again, and I couldn't see why the engineer didn't understand that. "I meant," I said with tremendous patience, "can you turn off the gravity in a given section? Like for instance the pilot's quarters? Because the pilot I'm bringing is a Faller, and he's been in gravity since we left Home Base. He'll never make it to Earth orbit if he has to do it in gravity."

Jamin made an impatient gesture, as if to brush away the problem. Looking at him, I wondered a trifle wildly whether he'd even make it to the *Marabou*.

The engineer sighed audibly over the Comm Link. "Well, hell, why didn't you say so? Ain't you never flown on a liner, lady? Naturally the bridge and the pilot's quarters can be set for freefall, and they usually are. How many liner pilots do you know who're Grounders?"

"Actually, I don't know any liner pilots except the one I'm bringing you."

"Well, I'm telling you, they're mostly Fallers. Why the hell would a Grounder want to fly?"

"I sometimes wonder why a Grounder would want to do anything."

"Me, too." The engineer sounded more sympathetic. I was apparently forgiven my stupidity in asking about the gravity generators.

"I don't want freefall quarters," Jamin said with frail authority.

"Why the hell not?" asked the engineer.

"I'm wondering," I added, staring at Jamin. He looked so worn that I'd tried to get him to spend the day in bed, but he knew we were likely to make contact with the *Marabou*, and he insisted on joining me in the cockpit.

"Collis," he said wearily. "Why else?"

"Collis can bunk with me. In gravity."

He looked surprised. "You'd do that?"

"What? Share quarters with your blue-eyed boy? I've been sharing my shuttle with him for some time now, and it doesn't seem to've done me any lasting harm."

"But you don't, I mean, you're not exactly," he said.

"What? Maternal? No, not exactly." I shrugged. "But this is entirely a matter of practical logistics. You have to be healthy to get the *Marabou* to Earth orbit. You have to have freefall for that. Collis can't take freefall, and you don't trust strange babysitters. Look, it's no big deal. I'd do the same for anyone my life depended on."

"I'm willing to bet that when we left Home Base, you'd have sooner risked your life than volunteered to share quarters with a six year old. It could ruin your reputation. You going soft, Skyrider?"

"Six year old? Skyrider?" said the *Marabou*'s engineer. "What the hell's going on over there? The Company said they'd send somebody, but—the Skyrider? And a six year old?"

"The six year old wasn't part of the plan," I said. "He's a sort of a bonus. At a small extra charge."

"That doesn't make sense," said the engineer. "You must be the Skyrider."

"Thanks. You mean you can tell straightaway, because I don't make sense?"

The engineer sounded a lot more confident all of a sudden. "It's a certain kind of not making sense." There was a grin in her voice. "Welcome, Skyrider."

"Jeez, I hope I live up to my reputation."

"I hope you live," Jamin said sourly.

"Thanks for the vote of confidence."

I had the *Marabou* on visual by then. She came up fast on the screens, a beautiful faceted gemstone glittering dully against a field of stars. Liners didn't make planetfall; they off-loaded passengers and supplies at space stations. They were built in space, and they stayed in space, and there was no need for streamlining to ward off atmosphere. To the eyes of an Earther, accustomed to vehicles constructed on the latest aerodynamic principles, she would probably have looked like an ungainly monster incapable of the speed and precision flying required of an interplanetary vessel. To my eyes, she was a beauty.

But at that moment I was much more concerned with the details of her docking facilities than with the splendor of her silhouette against the stars. The engineer and Jamin both waited in silence while I centered our screens on her shuttle dock and instructed the computer to augment.

At first glance, it looked good. On closer study, it still looked good. At maximum magnification, it looked good . . . at first. Then I saw the mark the military had made.

The engineer was impatient. "Well?"

I spoke without thinking. "Clumsy goddamn bastards."

She was silent a moment. "No good, huh?"

I studied the screen. "I don't know. Maybe."

More silence. "Damn it, give us an answer."

"They sheared off the aft hook and maybe part of the lock."

The silence was almost tangible.

I studied the screens. "I can try."

"You'd try?" She was afraid to hope . . . and afraid not to. "With one hook gone, and maybe part of the lock, you'd try anyway?"

"What've I got to lose?"

"Now I know you're the Skyrider. Your life is what you've got to lose, that's all."

"I don't s'pose my life's worth a lot more than yours."

"Mine's already forfeit."

"Not unless I say so, it isn't. That's the trouble with you people who want to live forever. You give up too easy. How can you have any fun if you back down from all the challenges that might keep you from living forever? And what's the good of living forever if you never have any fun?"

She thought that one over for a while. "You call this fun?"

"Well, it sure isn't boring."

CHAPTER EIGHTEEN

Collis came into the cockpit while I was calculating the "catch and match" routine. "You'd better hang onto your kid," I told Jamin.

"Maybe you should go strap down in your quarters," said Jamin.

"Do I have to?" asked Collis.

"No." I said it quickly, before Jamin could speak. The kid wouldn't be any safer neatly strapped down in his quarters. There were only two likely possibilities here: a perfect docking or sudden death. In a perfect docking, Collis would be as safe in the cockpit as in his quarters; and in the other eventuality, he wouldn't be safe anywhere. He and Jamin had put a lot of effort into staying together. This didn't seem like a sensible time to quit.

Jamin looked at me, and I could see him working

it out for himself. Pain and fatigue slowed his thinking, but apparently had no appreciable effect on his phenomenal courage. When he'd followed through my logic, he achieved a brave, frayed smile. "Right, as usual," he told me. To Collis he added, "How about sitting on my lap? You might as well have a ringside seat." In the early days of the trip he would have lifted Collis into his lap. Hell, in the early days of the trip he had gone so far as to carry me from the cargo hold to my quarters. Now he had trouble lifting a coffee cup.

Collis clambered into his lap unaided and turned to study the viewscreens with a cheerful interest born of merciful ignorance. Our "piloting" lessons hadn't progressed to the stage where he would recognize a damaged docking mechanism.

I didn't have to tell him to keep quiet. Nobody said anything while I concentrated on exactly matching speed and rotation with the *Marabou*. It took a while; her speed was constant, and so was her period of rotation, but there was a glitch in the system somewhere that made her pitch crazily at apparently random intervals. The monster had hiccups.

"What's that damned starboard pitch?" I demanded of the engineer.

Since the *Marabou* was shaped very like a faceted gemstone, with a flattened "top" and pointed "bottom" and a roughly spherical, symmetrical middle section, she actually had no port or starboard. Her engineer didn't question my terminology, and didn't tell me what caused the pitch; I didn't really want to know. Neither, however, did I want to know what I was told: "Can't be helped." I wanted to hear that the problem was caused by an oversight that could be easily corrected. We don't always hear what we'd like.

"Then we'll have to live with it," I said.

"I sure hope so," said the engineer.

"Hang on. I'm coming in."

I don't know whether she held on. Jamin and Collis certainly did. Which was as well, because the *Marabou* hiccupped just as we made contact.

One develops a sort of sixth sense about things like that. There was no way I could see it coming. Maybe I sensed it. At any rate, I reacted before I knew what I was reacting to. At exactly the instant of contact, instead of hitting the lock switches, which would have been the logical maneuver and would have killed us, I hit the reverse thrusters. If I hadn't, we might very well have sheared off the remaining hooks on the *Marabou* and would certainly have smashed fatally against her.

We were a kilometer away before I was consciously aware of the need to back off. And I'd hit the thrusters so hard that we were a kilometer farther away before my shaky manipulation of the controls resulted in a decrease and reverse of thrust. "Damn!" I said unsteadily.

The engineer said unexpectedly, "That was damn good flying."

"That was what you call a failure." I reminded myself what a good idea it was to breathe once in a while.

"You're alive, aren't you?" asked the engineer.

"We're not docked, are we?"

"Come off it." She sounded unutterably weary. "There's no way you can dock. You shouldn't even have tried. There's no damn sense in killing yourselves. If you quit now, you'll surely have enough fuel left to make Earth orbit."

"We'll try again."

"Damn it, why? To prove the great Skyrider doesn't quit?"

"I see her reputation really has preceded us," Jamin said with a smile.

"Talk her out of it," she said. "Isn't it enough that the military lost two good men? Do you have to kill yourselves, too?"

"I hadn't planned suicide." I was moving in on the *Marabou*, carefully matching again.

"Pilot?" said the engineer.

"I can't stop her," said Jamin.

"You could," I said. "But why would you? The sooner we dock, the sooner you get back into freefall."

"He can get freefall quarters at an Earth station," said the engineer.

"Look again, my friend," I said. "This is a Falcon. The Company moves in mysterious ways its wonders to perform. We can dock with a liner, or an asteroid, or on a flight deck. But not at a space station." We were almost matched again. "It's something I mean to correct about this shuttle when I get a chance, but I haven't had time."

"There'll be other liners in orbit," said the engineer. "You can dock with one of them. Or maybe they've got that new flight deck completed on Alpha Station."

"I didn't know they were planning one. We're docking with the *Marabou*."

"Don't be a damned fool. You can't dock with us."

I was ready to try, but I looked at Jamin before I started in this time. He was looking at me. I looked at Collis, back at Jamin, and waited. It was his kid. He knew the risks. The engineer was right; we could probably dock with something in Earth orbit, and we were risking the kid's life trying to dock with the *Marabou*.

"That's what we came here for, isn't it?" asked Jamin.

"Are you telepathic, or what?"

"Mostly what." He grinned wearily.

"*Defiance*, do you read me?" asked the engineer. "Don't try it again, damn it. You can't do it. Nobody could."

Jamin smiled to himself. "The Skyrider can." He sounded confident enough, but I noticed that when I put my hands on the controls to take us in again, he tightened his grip on Collis.

"No problem," I told the engineer, trying to sound as confident as Jamin had. "Just be sure you've got the gravity generator on the bridge turned off."

"It's off." She sounded dubious.

"Then hang onto your helmet. We're coming in."

The *Marabou* hiccupped. I slid the *Defiance* in quickly, before it could hiccup again. The controls responded perfectly. We glided in, bellied up to the dock, touched, and this time I hit the lock switches. The undamaged hooks slid home. I had worried that the hook damaged in the military effort might have jammed the whole mechanism or that if the hooks worked, the broken one might have an end bent enough to miss its matching hook on the *Defiance* and keep us from making a secure connection. It did neither. We waited, scarcely breathing, watching the readout to see if the lock would hold. It held. Even when the *Marabou* hiccupped again.

After a long moment the engineer broke our silence with a strangled laugh that sounded almost like a sob. "I really didn't think it could be done."

"No problem." I hoped my voice was steadier than my hands were.

"I see why they call you the Skyrider," she said.

"Listen, I only did this to earn my Falcon. Now send your people aboard to get your supplies, and get those damn engines fixed. It would be a shame to lose the mission now, after all this trouble." I stood up, grinning at Collis. "Come on, guy. Let's get your papa into freefall before he goes into shock."

Jamin released Collis and looked up at me with an odd little smile. "I'm already in shock."

Collis looked up at him quickly.

"He doesn't mean gravity shock," I said, and grinned at Jamin. "You called me hotshot."

He shrugged ineffably. "I was right, wasn't I?"

CHAPTER NINETEEN

While the engineers mended the *Marabou*, her freefall sections mended Jamin. He was young and hardy, and his recovery was quick. I had to work fast to get my extortion accomplished before he was well enough to realize what was going on.

It helped that Willem was his cousin. Willem had a lot of pull with the Company, and he had already displayed his concern for Jamin and Collis, when we first found the kid stowed away on the *Defiance*. Naturally, when I called Home Base on the Comm Link, I insisted on speaking first with Uluniu; she fancied herself an expert at awkward negotiations, and she outranked Willem. If I could bluff her, she'd turn me over to him, and from there I was home free.

"I beg your pardon?" That was her initial response. I solemnly swear it. The ambassador-at-large listened to my threats and demands, and she cleared her throat twice, and she said, "I beg your pardon?"

"I said, we've made the docking. Now we'll talk terms. We're willing to bring the liner in whole, passengers and payload, if you give us another Falcon, fully fueled and properly papered. Jamin never bartered with you before we left, so there's no agreement as to what his pay will be. This is what he wants. Also standard hazardous duty pay for the mission, and full coverage for any medical treatment he and/or his son may require or obtain before returning to the Belt. He's willing to make the same arrangement I've made about the use of his shuttle for Company runs. Are you getting all this down? We'll start spacing the cargo in twenty-four hours if we haven't had an affirmative answer from Home Base by that time. When it's all spaced, if we still haven't heard, we'll release from the *Marabou* and jump for Earth orbit. Shall I run through all that again?" I was enjoying myself.

Uluniu wasn't having quite so much fun. "I don't understand. It was clearly understood that Jamin was to receive hazardous duty pay for the mission. That was understood before you left."

"Understood by whom, I'm wondering? Listen, shall I run over it again, just to be sure you've got it straight? We want a shuttle, with fuel and papers, extra pay, and medical treatment. Did you get it down?"

"But I thought it was understood . . ."

"Maybe you want to discuss this with the other VIPs before you give me your answer."

"This is extortion. This is . . . Do you realize this is . . ."

"This is called *negotiating*. I don't know where you heard that other word, but it's nasty. I don't think you should repeat it over the Comm Link."

"Do the *Marabou* crew members realize what you're doing?"

"Sure, but how can they stop me? I have them at gunpoint." I grinned at the Comm-tech beside me, and he went into a little silent comic routine about the gun I wasn't aiming at him.

"All of them?" Uluniu sounded startled.

"Lady, you better believe it. I'm good."

That got the Comm-tech started again. He was a regular comedian.

"Piracy," said Uluniu. "Mutiny."

"Watch your language."

"I'll get back to you." She sounded faint.

"Make it hasty. For all I know, the *Marabou* crew is riddled with heroes. I don't want to have to hurt anyone."

She didn't answer that, and I cut the Link.

"Think they'll give in?" asked the Comm-tech.

I shrugged. "They'll give me the medical coverage. I don't know about the shuttle. I just threw it in for extra incentive."

"You're pretty sure of yourself, aren't you?"

I grinned. "Somebody has to be."

He ruffled his short red hair, leaving most of it standing on end. The look he gave me was half puzzled, half amazed. "Lady, from all I've heard since you came aboard, the whole damn universe seems to believe you can do 'most anything that strikes your fancy. But I don't get it. You just threw in the shuttle? What does that mean? You want some medical treatment for that pilot, and you want it enough to buck the whole Company to get it?''

''Not so much for the pilot as for his kid.''

''Is this the Skyrider talking? You're risking your neck for some kid?''

''Collis isn't just 'some kid.' I owe him.''

''I don't get it.''

''Nobody asked you to.''

He shook his head. ''Well, I'll let you know if they call you back.''

''If I'm not in my quarters, page me. I've got to talk to some Earthers, I think.''

He just shook his head, saying as clearly as if he'd used words that he didn't quite know what all the fuss was about; whatever else this Skyrider person was, she was crazy, and that was that.

I grinned at him and went in search of Earthers. Collis whirlwind-hugged me in the corridor outside our quarters and invited himself along. The kid hadn't had much to do since we'd boarded the *Marabou*, and I didn't feel like telling him I didn't want him along. Time he learned a little something about politics anyway. Maybe Jamin wouldn't approve if he knew, but Jamin wouldn't approve of much of anything I'd done since the docking. The main thing, as far as I could see, was not to let him know what I was doing till it was done. Which wasn't hard, since he wasn't yet up to coming out of his freefall quarters and I hadn't had time yet to visit him there.

Somebody had apparently found time to tell the passengers who I was. To most Earthers, my name, or any Belter's name, was a matter of indifference, and most of these had never heard of me before. But there were a few Colonials on board, and a couple of lower echelon high muckymuck Earthers who had heard the legends, and besides, I'd just given the whole lot of them a new chance at life. Even those who didn't know me from Adam, and under ordinary circumstances wouldn't want to, were pleased as pleased to meet me now. One stodgy Earther gentleman even asked for my autograph!

I gave him it, and wormed my way through the crowd in the passenger rec room, nodding and smiling till my face hurt, looking for familiar faces. I finally found Stockholder Washington, whose face was familiar mostly from newsfax. "Stockholder, could I talk with you for a moment?"

He looked at me blankly, then with mild interest, and eventually with amused surprise. "Are you the Skyrider?"

I was getting just a little tired of that look and that question. Several of the Earthers I'd met and every individual on the *Marabou*'s crew had given me that look and asked that question. My reputation may have preceded me, but apparently my description hadn't, and whatever they'd all expected, I wasn't it.

"You were expecting maybe God?" I asked wearily.

To my surprise, his look of amusement changed from superior to delighted, and he laughed right out loud. "I guess maybe I was, at that." He sobered, studying my face. "You look like all this"—he gestured toward my swarming admirers—"isn't exactly what you expected, either. Need a drink?" Apparently we were going to be buddies. No small gesture from a man of his political stature.

"More like a little privacy," I said. "But that can wait. We've got to talk. And—are there any media people on board? Newsfax, and that?"

Puzzled amusement again, with overtones of disapproval. Maybe we wouldn't be buddies, after all. "Quite a number of them, actually. But are you certain you don't already have publicity enough?"

"More than enough. It's not for me. It's . . . well . . . important. If you could collect any media personnel and any other high m— I mean . . ."

"Muckymucks?" He was considering whether we could still be buddies. His lips weren't smiling, but his eyes were. A neat trick, if you can do it.

"Such as yourself," I agreed. "And bring them to, um . . . where can we meet? Is there a smaller rec room, or a briefing room, or something?"

"I think I could manage a briefing room," he said judiciously. "What's this all about, if I might ask?"

"It's . . . important." I wasn't very good at this part. "Just, I don't want to have to go through it all twice, could you just believe me that it's important and do it?"

He frowned: the compleat politician considering an unexpected proposal. "You repeat that 'it,' whatever 'it' may be, is important. To whom, if I might ask?"

"To . . . to all of us. Not just here, but . . . Look, I know I'm no good at this kind of thing. I can't give a rousing good speech and, space, I mean, I'm just a pilot, that's why, but I mean, it's . . . it's important.''

"So you've told me." He considered it some more. "Briefing room Beta Four, crew level Three, at oh nine hundred Standard. Will that do?"

I grinned my relief. "That's wonderful. Thank you, Stockholder.''

He nodded dubiously and turned away.

"Look, Skyrider," said Collis. "These guys have an electronic Planets, with a three-color board and everything."

I looked. "These guys" were a pair of freckle-faced teenagers, Earth-kine by the look of them, whose pale eyes widened at sight of me and who both said at once, in tones of doubt and wonder, "You're the Skyrider?"

"I'm the Skyrider." My voice sounded as weary as I felt. I tried to lighten it with a brief smile before I turned to Collis. "That's nice, kid, but let's get out of here, okay? We've got things to do."

"Like what?" He didn't move away from the Earther boys, who were too busy staring to say anything.

"Like talking to the captain of this monster."

"Talking to the captain? What about?" He still sounded rebellious, but his curiosity was aroused. He followed me . . . or tried to. We were both trapped by the partying throng, most of whom had forgotten me by now; they were just busy having a good old time. It was pleasant to be out of the limelight again, but I was unnerved by the sheer number of people, even though they were no longer paying me any attention.

I bumped into a squat little gentleman who, as a result, spilled his drink all over my flight suit and frowned blearily around without noticing me for a moment.

"Bother!" I tried to edge past him, but there was a broad-bottomed lady on one side of him and a long, thin, gesticulating fellow on the other, neither of whom made any move to make way for passersby. "Space *and* bother." I reminded myself firmly that it would be a really bad plan to start a brawl in there. But I despaired of getting out by any other means.

"There's another way out, over here," said Collis.

We were out of the crowded rec room in minutes. Kids are like that. Turn one loose in an interesting new environment, and no matter how complex it is, he'll have all the back corridors memorized before bedtime. He may not be able to find a given area by the normal routes, but he'll know three shortcuts to the backdoor.

When I got the rec room door shut behind us, silence descended like a protecting blanket around us. We were in a homey metal and plastic corridor, and I was completely lost. "Which way to the captain's quarters from here?" I asked.

Collis looked at me in surprise. "Are you lost?"

"Absolutely. Are you?"

"Nope." He grinned in pleased superiority and led the way unerringly to the captain's quarters, two levels down and all the way across the ship from the rec room where I'd found Stockholder Washington.

I hadn't met the captain before and wasn't sure what to expect. Her quarters didn't give much of a clue. On a liner, the captain's primary responsibility is the payload, which usually consists of more Earthers than anything else, so it might not mean much that her quarters were decorated in Earther woods and fabrics. She answered the door like a Belter, on her feet and ready for anything, but she had the gravity set for Mars. Her costume was standard Interplanetary Captain's uniform; no clue there. Her English, when she greeted us, was Company-perfect.

"Sorry I haven't had time to pay you an official visit," she said straightaway. "You've probably been told I was ill when you docked with us. That wasn't strictly true." She touched the back of her head and grinned ruefully. "My loyal crew is reluctant to admit I let those damn dirt-eaters (I beg your pardon, I mean the passengers) catch me by surprise in their hysterical rebellion when the engines first blew. This is the first day the med-techs have let me out of bed since then." She gestured toward chairs and invited us to sit. "So you're the Skyrider. And you must be our new pilot's son. Collis, is it?"

"Yes, sir," said Collis.

"How's your dad doing? Better now that he's in freefall?" She looked at me, not waiting for his answer. "That was a damned foolhardy stunt he pulled, coming all the way out here in gravity. What was he trying to prove, anyway? I've heard he's a hell of a pilot, but how smart can he be if he pulls a stunt like that?"

Collis answered her before I could figure out what

to say. "It was my fault, sir. I'm allergic to freefall, and I stowed away on the *Defiance*." He glanced at me, then looked steadily back at her. "I didn't know it would hurt him."

She covered her surprise very nicely. "That explains it, then. Maybe after this he'll have sense enough not to keep secrets from you." She awarded him an efficient smile and turned back to me. "I understand you're holding us hostage. Want to tell me about it?"

"Not particularly. That's not what I came here to see you about."

She studied me a moment and decided to smile. "You do understand I'm just a figurehead here?"

"A little more than that, I think, Captain," I said.

She nodded. "Okay. I think we understand each other . . . for the moment, anyway."

"Were you in the war?"

Her brows lifted ever so slightly. "Yes."

"Which side?"

"I see." She looked wary.

"I don't think you do, sir. Let me rephrase my question. If war broke out today, which side would you be on? Colonial or Earth?"

"That would depend on the circumstances, wouldn't it?" It wasn't really a question.

"I don't think so, sir."

Her lips quirked in the hint of a smile. "For the sake of argument, let's say—just hypothetically, mind you—that I'd be on the side of the Colonies."

"Then there'd be no reason to argue."

The smile became more obvious. "I thought not."

I didn't say anything till the smile finally faltered. "You want to stop playing games now?" I asked then.

"Games?"

I shrugged. "Okay. It's your ship. Die with it." To Collis, I said thoughtfully, "I've got a meeting to attend in about an hour. That gives us time to go talk to your papa and start getting the *Defiance* ready for separation."

The captain stared. "Separation?"

Rising, I nodded at her and reached for Collis's hand. "That's right, Captain Yee. Separation. I like living. Come on, kid."

"Wait a minute." She could manage a tone of authority when she wanted to. We paused, and I looked back at her expectantly. "What are you trying to pull?" She wasn't even thinking about smiling now.

I shrugged again. "Ain't me, sir. It's the Earthers. But you'll know that already."

"Know *what*, damn it?"

"Didn't they let you in on the plan? I thought even Earthers would ask for voluntary sacrifices, at least among their officers."

She shook her head slowly. "Nobody asked for a sacrifice. Nobody's *be*ing sacrificed . . . as far as I know."

"Maybe you don't know enough."

"Maybe I don't."

I studied her. My job would be a lot easier if I had her cooperation, and that of her crew.

"You want to tell me, or am I supposed to guess?" she asked.

223

"I think maybe you have guessed, already."

She hesitated. "The Patrol sent us rookies."

"I thought as much. But I have to be . . . I think I'd best be a trifle wary, here. There's only one of me. You've got a crew of twenty."

"It's not a contest . . . yet."

"That's all I'd ask for. Listen, I really don't want to tell the whole story twice, and I've got a bunch of people ready to listen at oh nine hundred. I think you and your crew, however many of them are free then, might want to hear what I have to say."

"They've just about got the engine repaired." She looked at the far bulkhead, shifted her weight, and looked at me. "It isn't over, though, is it?"

"I don't think it is."

"They knew you'd make the docking."

"Let's say I think they were prepared for that eventuality, yes."

"We have no weapons."

"The *Defiance* has."

"You have a plan?"

"Not much of one, but it's the best I can do."

"Name the place. We'll be there."

I named it.

CHAPTER TWENTY

First I had to deal with the Company, but that didn't take long. Uluniu had talked to Willem, and it was Willem who returned my call. He stood firm about the Falcon—no deal—but readily agreed to the medical coverage. I'd only thrown in the Falcon to give him something to refuse me, so I gave him only a token argument before I got the medical guarantee firmly on record and released my "hostages," most of whom never even knew they'd been "held."

Stockholder Washington came through with a dozen or so media personnel and several high muckymucks for the meeting. One of them was such a high muckymuck that I wondered how she happened to be on that doomed flight, but maybe she was out of favor with the ruling group, or maybe she'd just been extremely unlucky. The planners would have made sure there were a few prominent persons on board just for verisimilitude, but there were limits. Besides, most of the people present were on board more or less by accident.

Captain Yee produced seven or eight crew members, including herself. They were a quieter, more serious group than the newspeople or the muckymucks. They probably had a much better idea why I'd called the meeting.

Everybody got quiet when I started laying out the story for them. Most of them were more grim than serious by the time I'd told everything that happened since Jamin and I first heard of the *Marabou*. I didn't leave much of anything out, and it didn't make a very pretty picture.

Jamin wasn't quite ready yet to brave the rigors of gravity so we'd run a direct intercom between his quarters and the briefing room, and we kept it open throughout. I brought Collis with me; he hadn't anything better to do. That turned out to be as well; after the speech there was a question-and-answer period, and the highest muckymuck there, a Board Adviser Brown, asked Collis more questions than she asked of me or Jamin.

He didn't know why I'd called the meeting, but he knew what had gone on since we started our plans to leave Home Base, and he had good stage presence. He answered Brown's questions seriously and simply, innocently filling in facts and suppositions I'd been hesitant about because they were politically touchy. He'd put the pieces together, too, and eventually asked her the question I'd been afraid to ask: "I see why they didn't warn most of these people, Board Adviser Brown, but I don't see how it could be anybody but Earthers that did all this, because the Colonials wouldn't do it this way and anyway they were so surprised and stuff, so, but why didn't they warn you? Because aren't you pretty important to be killed with the rest of us?''

Dead silence followed that. Board Adviser Brown eventually cleared her throat and looked from Collis to the rest of us. She'd been trying to find some way or reason to disbelieve my whole story, or at least my conclusions about it, but her own answer was the clincher. ''My advisers did try to warn me, in a way. They refused to book my passage on this flight. I was supposed to stay on Mars for another silly charity ball.'' She blinked, looked uncomfortable, and smiled wryly. ''I've always hated those damn things. I'm afraid I'm playing hookey, Collis. I sneaked away and booked my own passage, without telling anyone.'' She looked at me. ''I wondered why they were so damned intent on keeping me there. I thought it must be some political undercurrent I'd missed. They know how much I hate those balls. Usually they get me out of that kind of duty when I ask.''

''Jamin,'' Captain Yee said suddenly, ''did that Colonial Starbird pilot make any attempt at communication before he opened fire on you?''

''None,'' said Jamin.

She turned to me. ''And you say he sounded surprised that you were on a rescue mission?''

''He wasn't just surprised. He didn't believe me.''

''But he did know about the *Marabou*. And thinking you were coming to attack us, he called you 'Earther.' ''

"That's right."

"We had talked on the Comm Link with . . . someone I knew during the war. We picked up a signal shortly after the Patrol's idiotic attempt to dock with us. Those poor rookies . . ." She looked pensive a moment, then grim. "Anyway, I told this . . . friend . . . this Colonial friend, that the Patrol had sent inexperienced pilots. We talked about it." She looked around at the crowd. "Speculating. Trying to understand."

Board Adviser Brown smiled in bleak sympathy. "You'd have been fools *not* to suspect the government after that failed attempt, Captain. I think we can all see that now."

"That's *if* you believe this whole paranoid romance," said a man behind Brown. He was one of the newspeople, and he had been recording the entire meeting, but this was the first time he'd contributed anything.

Brown turned sedately to examine him; a long, appraising scrutiny. "Are we to take it, then, that you *don't* believe some part of what we've been told here this morning, Mr. Jenski?" she asked politely.

"I don't believe any of it." He was uncomfortable under her steady gaze, but he didn't back down. "Who ever heard such nonsense? A pilots' brawl, a mishap with some medication, a supposedly murdered babysitter—and you admit she was an Earther," he added, staring defiantly at me, daring me to deny it. "Yet you maintain that the villains of the piece are Earthers, themselves. Have you any reasonable explanation as to why they would kill one of their own?"

"Look at yourself," said Brown.

"I beg your pardon," said Jenski.

"You assume that since the babysitter was an Earther, her assassin must have been a Colonial."

"Naturally. It's only logical."

"There's your reason," said Brown.

"Space him," said Yee. "We're overlooking something here."

Brown turned her inquiring dark gaze to Yee. "The final attack?"

"I beg your pardon?" said Jenski.

Yee ignored him. "Just so. They knew the Skyrider would make the docking. Now, no matter who we think might be behind all this, it's pretty clear someone is. Ships don't sabotage themselves. Bombs don't grow by spontaneous magic."

"They don't grow by spontaneous anything," said another newsperson. "Somebody planted them. And you think the same somebody is coming after us again? Now? Because the Skyrider did succeed in docking with us?"

"It's conceivable," said Yee.

Jamin finally asked the question I should have remembered to ask a long time ago. "Captain Yee, just what is this payload that's so important to the Company that Insurrectionists would supposedly be willing to go to these lengths to keep it from reaching Earth?"

"There is no payload," said Yee, "except the passengers."

The silence that followed that announcement was deafening. Only Jamin was sufficiently self-possessed to ask, politely, that she elaborate.

"There's nothing more to tell, really," she said. "We were assigned a payload. Something scientific; I don't even know what it was. United Industries commissioned its passage. And then, at the last minute, they refused to load. Their representative made some space-happy fuss about the dimensions of our cargo holds and the quality of our gravity generators. I thought it odd at the time, but not odd enough to abort the run."

"United Industries is a Company offshoot, isn't it?" someone asked.

"With strong ties to the Patrol," said someone else.

"People, I think it's pretty obvious what we're up against here," said Brown. "The question is, what are we going to do about it?"

"We're going to survive," said Yee.

"I'm afraid I don't quite see how," said Brown.

"We have no weapons," said a crew member.

"We have the Skyrider," said Collis.

Brown looked indulgent. "And she's a fine warrior, young man. But even the Skyrider has her limitations."

"We also have the *Defiance*," said Jamin.

"You people are serious," said Jenski.

"You noticed," I said.

"But this is ridiculous," said Jenski.

"Maybe," I said.

"Earther," muttered a crew member.

I shrugged. "They don't have to work quite so hard at staying alive. It's really not surprising that they sort of forget how to think things through."

"I beg your pardon," said Jenski.

"No, you don't," I said.

"Space the man," said Yee. "We need a plan."

"We aren't under attack yet," said someone.

"We'll be ready to run in a few hours," said someone else.

"Meantime, we're sitting ducks if anybody does attack," said Yee.

"I've got the sensors rigged through to my quarters," said Jamin. "The Skyrider will have time to kick free."

"And I have weapons on the *Defiance*," I said.

"Depending on what comes after us . . ." began Yee.

"If anything," said Jenski.

". . . your weapons may help," said Yee. "But there's a limit to what you can do with just one Falcon, even if it is armed."

"We could call for help," said Brown.

"From whom?" I asked.

She looked at me. "Oh." After a moment she smiled wryly. "I guess you're right about us Earthers. We do forget to think things through." No wonder the woman was a Board Adviser.

Yee turned to a member of her crew. "How much is left of the engine you tore down to mend the other?"

He considered it, frowning. "Not much. The fuel pods are intact. Beyond that it's just scrap metal."

231

"Will you need that fuel to make Earth orbit?" I asked.

Yee shook her head. "We're not that far insystem yet. The fuel systems are redundant, for safety. If we'd gone farther insystem before the repairs were completed, I planned to use the spare pods to see if we could get enough boost to get back out. But we won't need them now."

The crew member beside her was deep in thought. "We'd have to be maneuverable," he said. "I can rig them and eject them. But the *Marabou* herself would have to be the propellant."

I saw what he was getting at. "Properly speaking, inertia would be the propellant, and the *Marabou* would be the guidance system."

He shook his head. "Inertia can hardly be called a—"

"Space that," said Yee. "Let's assume we'll be maneuverable. That means we can aim them and throw them. How will you detonate them?"

"That's easy. Liquid malite is highly unstable. And they are still liquid: I checked that this morning. It would solidify pretty quickly if the pods were broached, but I think I can rig an impact-sensitive explosive to each pod, so if it connects with an enemy ship, it will blow, and that will blow the malite before it can solidify."

"It's an interesting problem," said another crew member. "I did some experiments with liquid malite in engineering school, and I found . . ."

"Get on it, both of you," Yee interrupted. "Anybody else got any bright ideas to contribute?"

232

Nobody had. The two liquid malite experts left the briefing room, their quiet but animated discussion cut off abruptly by the closing door behind them, and we were left in silence.

"Mostly I just wanted all of you to know what's on," I said. "If we make Earth orbit, I'd be glad just not to be alone with this information. I don't know what I intend to do with it, particularly if we're *not* attacked again before we get this monster home. Now at least it's not my sole responsibility." I hesitated over that, but couldn't think of a better way to phrase it. "Anyway, now you know. And I'd best go check out the *Defiance* and get her ready for separation. Just in case."

"Can I go with you?" asked Collis.

"No," said Jamin.

I looked helplessly at Collis. To my surprise, it was Captain Yee who came to my aid. "I understand you're confined to gravity, young man," she said.

Collis blushed. "Yes, sir."

"Then the place you'll be most useful is *in* gravity. You can help with the passengers, if it's okay with your dad. I'll assign you duty with Ensign Stepanovich. It's his job to instruct the passengers on proper procedure in case of emergency maneuvers or loss of gravity. Think you could help with that?"

"Oh, yes, please, sir." Collis stood straighter, with his chest thrust out and his shoulders back in what he must have imagined to be proper military posture.

"At ease, soldier," said Yee. "Okay with you, Jamin?"

He really hadn't any choice. "Okay. Be good, Collis."

Collis stiffened, blushing again. "Papa," he said impatiently.

I winked at him. "Fathers will be fathers."

"Let's get to work here, crewman," said Stepanovich.

Collis grinned at me and followed Stepanovich out.

"I think," said Brown, "that we'd do well to follow the boy's example by making ourselves useful in our chosen fields. I don't see much immediate need for a political adviser, but you newspeople could surely find useful activities. Our fellow passengers have a right to know, if and when the time comes, what's going on and why. They might be placated, in the event of an attack, by a kind of running commentary, if any of you have experience with that sort of thing? There's nothing more demoralizing than to know that one is surrounded by great danger without updated information as to what and how great the danger is."

"Good idea," said Yee. "Ensign Bates, get volunteers on that if you can, and set them up with the intercom equipment."

"Somebody should record the event, if it comes, for later evidence," said Brown.

"Get on that, Kruger," said Yee.

"And I suppose I *could* contact Earth," said Brown.

"Think you could get us any support?" asked Yee.

Brown shook her head. "I don't know. I really

don't know. My God. Who the hell do you trust in a situation like this?''

"I don't know," said Yee. "You'll have to be the judge of that."

The engine came unexpectedly to life at that moment, with a barely perceptible, almost subliminal rumble that I perceived less with my ears than through the soles of my feet. Captain Yee punched an intercom button. "Engineers, you're ahead of schedule."

"Listen to her sing!" said a disembodied voice through the speaker.

"I hear her. Can she maneuver?"

The voice sounded a little less exuberant. "I think so, Captain. But she'll wallow.''

Yee looked at Jamin's image on another screen. "Pilot, are you prepared to assume command?"

I left them to their formal ritual; even with one engine brought back to life, the *Marabou* couldn't fight off an attack without help from the *Defiance* . . . and the gods. The odds were against us if the Earthers sent out any real force. The only advantage we had, if it could be called an advantage, was that they would be depending (I hoped) on an element of surprise that no longer existed.

The *Defiance* seemed empty with Jamin and Collis gone. I punched up the Comm Link connection to the *Marabou*'s bridge, and Jamin's pale face stared out of the screen at me. The *Marabou* had quit hiccupping. "Anything show on your screens yet?" I asked.

He shook his head. "Negative. I have the long-range scanners on. Don't disengage till I give you the signal; no sense wasting fuel. You'll have plenty of time to get clear if you wait till I spot them.''

"Just be sure you do spot them. I wouldn't like to be sitting out here like a beginner's mark when they come in range.''

"You sound pretty sure they're coming.''

"Aren't you?''

"I guess I am.'' He looked away from the screen, checking the scanners. "You could make a run for Earth, Skyrider. You could tell them what happened, anyway.''

"Don't think the thought hadn't crossed my mind. But they'll know what happened, Jamin.''

"We won't be around to tell them.''

"They don't need told. And don't be so sure we won't be around. We've both been in tight spots before, and we're still here to argue about it.''

He grinned. "Once a hero, always a hero.''

"I ain't no hero. I'm a realist. We have a chance.''

"We have two jury-rigged fuel pod bombs, a laser, and a photar. They'll probably send a squad of fighters. You call that a chance?''

"Don't forget that Starbird we met on the way in.''

He stared. "What in space has that got to do with anything?''

I shrugged. "Maybe nothing. Maybe everything. Check your scanners.''

He checked. "Clear so far. You think he followed us?''

"It's a chance.'' I'd been running a systems check while we talked, and settled back with relief when all systems checked okay. I switched off the gravity and tugged my shock webbing a little tighter. "Scanners still clear?"

"So far."

"They won't wait much longer. They probably have a pretty good idea how much time they'd have between our docking and the *Marabou*'s repair."

"Why would they hurry? She's defenseless. They've got all the time in the world."

"Not if they want it to look like an Insurrectionist attack. For that they've got to hit us while we're still well out from Earth. They won't want spectators."

"We have the Comm Link, anyway. But I suppose, if your Earther theory is correct—"

"You doubt it?"

He shrugged. "If it's correct, they'll jam the Comm Link."

"You really still think it might be Insurrectionists?"

A wry smile turned up the corners of his mouth. "I don't really care who it is. If we're attacked at all, it won't much matter if it's Earthers or Insurrectionists or little green men from another galaxy. We'll be just as defenseless."

"Check your scanners."

He checked, and even over the Link I could see his jaw set. "Squadron coming in. Looks like Starbirds, but I don't yet have a clear ident. Coordinates oh three hundred, three thirty, just on the edge of scanner range. Disengage. I repeat, disengage. Prepare for attack." He was feeling out his controls, not moving yet, giving me plenty of room to maneuver. "All personnel to emergency stations on the double."

237

I could hear the order echo over the *Marabou*'s intercom system.

When I switched the screen from Comm Link to scanners, it didn't show a sign of the intruders. The *Defiance* slid obediently away from the *Marabou* and I hit the thrusters hard. Maybe I could get far enough out of range to double back and catch their tails by surprise. It was a slim hope, but all we had were slim hopes.

The starry silence of space enveloped us. The *Marabou* was a distant flicker of light and dark against the Milky Way. The *Defiance* whispered and sang in the dark. When her scanners finally picked up the enemy squadron, they were already near enough for the *Marabou* to make a positive ID. Her Comm Link chattered static, and I heard the message go out to Earth: "Interplanetary liner *Marabou* in trouble. Please assist. We are under attack by a squadron of Colonial Starbirds." The nearest Starbird sent a bolt of deadly lightning across the dark, toward the *Marabou*. "I repeat, we are under attack by Colonial Starbirds. Please assist. Interplanetary—"

The Link went dead.

CHAPTER TWENTY-ONE

The "Insurrectionists" had waited till they heard the *Marabou*'s distress call before they jammed the Link. They were taking a chance, and they couldn't wait to let the call be repeated; it wouldn't have been worded quite the same way the second time. By then they were close enough to be correctly identified. The bright new paint jobs on those Starbirds were too sloppy to stand up to close inspection. They were Patrol ships, and at close range the Patrol insignia showed clearly through the Colonial emblem.

Jamin might have been a little clumsy with the *Defiance*, but he handled the *Marabou* with such delicate perfection that she looked like a dancer. The Starbirds came at her in a cluster, and she pivoted and ran so neatly that not one of them got a clean shot at her. They came around, weapons blazing, and she dived straight out of the line of fire, turned end over end in a beautiful curve that brought her up facing them, and Jamin must have poured all her power into the leap she made toward them.

They peeled off nervously, but I saw the blip on my scanner when the engineers released the first of their fuel pod bombs, and the Starbird they'd aimed it at waltzed right into it. The *Marabou*, meantime, curved up and away from the scattered Starbirds, while the fuel pod continued on her original path, so not only did the Starbird never know what hit it, but the others couldn't figure it out, either.

Now, however, they were divided, and coming at the *Marabou* from two directions. None of them had noticed me yet. They thought they had the *Marabou* at their mercy, and one unexpected casualty wasn't enough to scare them off. I hit the thrusters and the laser controls both at once. There was no chance of hitting them at that range, but I had plenty of firepower, and the shock value of my blazing weapons was well worth the wasted power.

I got them off the *Marabou*, anyway. They seemed to hesitate over my arrival, puzzling it out. But it didn't take them long to recognize the obvious: the *Marabou* had no real weapons. I had. She could wait while they dealt with me.

Their mistake. Jamin whipped her around and headed straight for us, waiting until the last possible second before pulling up. I didn't see the blip that time, but I saw the explosion. If he'd had four more fuel pod bombs, he might not even have needed me.

Unfortunately, that shot had exhausted his store.
And I had four Starbirds gunning for me. Obviously
startled by this second inexplicable casualty, all four
of them shot wild the first time around. I singed
one's wing, but it didn't even slow him down. They
spat by on both sides of me, their exhausts flaring,
and out of the corner of my eye I saw both pairs
separating as they went by.

I flipped the *Defiance* over, letting her ride
backward, away from the Starbirds, with her nose
pointed the way we had come. The Starbirds curved
away from me in four directions before they flipped
over. It left them at awkward angles for firing at me,
but it wouldn't take them long to remedy that, and
the real point was that it left me at the center of a
deadly four-petaled flower. Once they angled back
for firing, there was no way all four of them could
miss—and no way I could hit all four. I could maybe
take one or two, if I was quick, but not four.

I kicked in the jockey thrusters, jumping sideways.
The Earthers were good. They held the formation and
stayed with me, and they were pulling their noses
toward me for firing. I cut in the thrusters, hoping to
dive right through them. I made it, too, but they
flipped over and kept coming. I was still at the
center of their formation, and nothing I tried could
shake them. The best I could do was to keep them
moving so they could never get a good enough angle
to fire.

They figured that out all too quickly. One of them
peeled away, and the remaining three spread out to
cover me. The one that had pulled away would presum-

ably pull back far enough to disregard my dodging, wait till he got an angle, and blow me to hell and gone.

In theory, three ships aren't enough to surround one in space. In practice, if one is flying a Falcon and the three ships chasing are Starbirds, three is a pretty effective number. They couldn't kill me, but they could keep me busy while the fourth one did the job.

I hit the thrusters again and angled as I went by so I could take a snap shot at one of them. It missed, but he skittered sideways anyway. I flipped the *Defiance* and threw a wild shot at one of the others while retreating tail-first, trying to catch that fourth bird in my laser screen. I couldn't find him, but he found me.

The deflector shield saved me. But it took a direct hit and burned out in an eerie green incandescent glory around me. I still couldn't see the ship that had fired. I skidded sideways and his second shot went past me. That gave away his position. I jockeyed for a shot at him, and missed. The others were coming at me again. The time I'd wasted on the fourth one had given them a chance to get an angle on me. All three fired at once. One of them was a little off with his aim. That was the one that caught me. The other two shots burst against each other in a blinding red fury, exactly where I had been a fraction of a second before. But I jockeyed right into the third one, and it caught the *Defiance* at a glancing angle that took out half her controls. She shook with the impact, screaming like a live thing. The whole cockpit spat short-circuiting sparks, and two of my scanners went dead. The air stank of burnt insulation. The computer chattered nonsense, collected itself, and began studiously to list its damages.

I slammed the jockeystick sideways, and nothing happened. Cursing, I hit the thrusters and we dived head-on toward one of the Starbirds. The Gypsies were singing, but the fizzle of dying electronic connections was all I was listening to. My own sweet Falcon, broken. Something was wrong with the air-filter system. Maybe the smoke or debris had clogged it. The cockpit air wasn't clearing as it ought to; it was thinning. And what was left reeked of mechanical death.

Maybe I went a little crazy. Jamin claimed afterward that I must have done. I don't clearly recall exactly what I did, much less why. Maybe the thin air affected my reasoning. Maybe it was just pure rage. Apparently, I tried to ram the Starbirds. I remember chasing one of them. . . .

Fortunately for all of us, my wild notion about the real Colonial we'd met on the way to the *Marabou* turned out not to be so wild after all. He'd taken my message home with him, brought his buddies, and trailed after us to the *Marabou*. If we docked with her, they wouldn't interfere. If we attacked, they'd have knocked us out of space and saved her themselves.

They had watched us dock on their long-range scanners, and they'd started home satisfied, when they picked up the fake Colonials lying in wait outside the *Marabou*'s scanner range. Curious, the real Colonials had waited. They had to stay at a considerable distance to keep the Earthers or us from picking them up. And they had to refuel, which meant a bigger ship out from Mars that had to maintain an even greater distance. When the Earthers attacked us, the last of the Colonials had just refueled and was returning to their waiting position. The distance was what took them so damn long.

I didn't know the battle was over till I heard Jamin shouting at me. "Skyrider, answer me! *Marabou* calling the *Defiance*, please respond. Skyrider!" The sound of his voice filtered slowly into my consciousness. I didn't quite understand why the Comm Link worked. Maybe it was a complicated Earther trick?

Dubious, I punched on the transmitter and said, "Jamin?"

"Thank the gods," he said. But there was a Colonial angling, I thought, to fire on him.

"Look out." I struggled with my no longer responsive *Defiance*, skating sideways and fighting a tendency to tumble, in an effort to find an angle from which I could fire on the Starbird without hitting the *Marabou*.

The Starbird, perhaps sensing my intention, drifted gracefully nearer the *Marabou*. "Hold your fire," said Jamin. "That's a real Colonial."

I blinked at my wavering scanner screens and peered out the visual screen to see if the unaugmented view was better. It was. I was close enough to have all six Starbirds on straight visual.

Six? "The bastards called in reinforcements," I said.

"Those are Colonials, Skyrider. Hold your fire," said Jamin.

I got the angle I wanted and had my finger on the firing stud when something in Jamin's tone finally got through to me. "What?"

It was one of the Starbird pilots who answered me. "The Earthers are gone, Melacha. The battle's over. We'll see you safely into orbit, but you'd better dock that cripple before she gives up on you."

The voice was familiar. My head hurt. I became distantly aware of the Gypsies singing. A warning klaxon howled in my ears.

"Melacha, do you read me? The battle's over," said the familiar voice. "If you can still dock that crate, you'd better do it."

"Michael?"

"Skyrider, dock," said Jamin.

"Where'd you come from?" I asked, still staring at the six Colonial Starbirds. They were dancing attendance to the *Marabou,* their bright Colonial paint jobs unmarred by any sign of Patrol insignia underneath.

"Just dock," said the Colonial, his voice suddenly weary.

"I don't know whether I can."

"Engage your synch system," said Jamin.

I hadn't thought of that. Dead-dockings were becoming a habit with me. "Oh. Sure." I reached for the control—or tried to. Nothing happened. Puzzled, I

245

looked down at the arm that didn't respond. It was the same one I'd injured in the explosion when we were leaving Home Base. It had been healing so efficiently on its own that I'd never found time to ask the *Marabou*'s med-techs to finish the job. Now, apparently, I'd torn the wound open again in the heat of battle. My flight suit was stained, and the arm hung useless at my side, dripping blood from my fingers onto the deck. "Damn," I said.

"What is it?" asked Jamin.

"Oh," I said, remembering belatedly where I was and what I was supposed to be doing.

"Your synch system is functioning, isn't it?" asked the Colonial. He sounded oddly anxious, as if he really cared what happened to me.

"I don't know." I manipulated the controls with my working hand and peered at the computer board to see its response.

"Skyrider, are you all right?" asked Jamin.

"Sure. No problem." I couldn't read the computer screen. But it didn't seem very important. "Synch system engaged. I think."

"You *think*?" said Jamin.

"Melacha," said the Colonial.

"I just can't read the damn board," I said impatiently.

"Then let me synch for you," said the Colonial.

I shook my head dizzily, forgetting he couldn't see me. "Don't crowd me."

"It's okay," said Jamin. "My computer's locked onto her signal."

"Okay, but is she sending the right data?"

"Course I am," I said. "It's my Falcon."

"Your Falcon has a hole in the starboard side you could put a Starbird through," said the Colonial.

"Skyrider, did your synch system klaxon sound?"

"I don't know. Something did."

"I can synch for her," said the Colonial.

"Leave me alone, damn it," I said. "I'm going in."

I did it, too. I don't know why I was so intent on doing it myself, aside from the obvious fact that if my synch system *was* working okay, it would bring me in a lot more smoothly than a hookup through the Colonial's Starbird. I wasn't thinking that clearly, though. Probably I was just being defiantly—and dangerously—independent, as usual.

Anyway, I lucked out. The synch system was working fine. We bellied up to the *Marabou* with perfect ease, despite all the jammed controls that had given me so much trouble toward the end of the battle, and the last thing I remembered afterward was throwing the lock switches to complete the docking.

Med-techs came on board to carry me back to the *Marabou*, where they used the liner's extensive facilities to put me back together again, more quickly and completely than nature had done on the way in from Home Base. The next thing I was consciously aware of was an anxious cherub leaning over me.

His father had braved the rigors of gravity to be there with us when I woke this time. "Who's minding the store?" I asked.

"The computer," said Jamin. "How do you feel?"

I sat up, stretching cautiously. "Is the *Defiance* okay?"

"She will be. How do you feel?"

I remembered the battle, and grinned. "Lucky." Then I remembered something else, and frowned at him. "Did I dream it, or were there real Colonials out there?"

"You didn't dream it." While I swung my legs over the edge of the bed and carefully stood up, he told me how the Colonials had followed us, and waited when they saw the Earther squadron, and come to our rescue when the Earthers attacked. "But about all they had to do was mopping up; you had those Earthers running scared."

"I had?"

"What would you do if a lone warrior in a crippled Falcon started trying to ram four Starbirds?"

"Panic, I guess." I flapped my arms experimentally. They both felt fine.

"You tried, literally, to ram them. You kept trying for a collision course, and you damn near made it a time or two. What did you think you were doing?"

I sat on the edge of the bed and grinned. "I don't remember. It worked, didn't it?"

"It worked. The Earthers didn't know what the hell to do. They were so busy dodging, most of their shots went wild."

"So what happened, finally?"

"The Colonials wiped them out."

"Just like that?"

"Just like that. They never knew what hit them."

"And we have no proof they were Earthers."

Jamin shrugged. "We may have it on holofilm, and there may be some identifiable debris. The Colonials are looking for it."

"What have you told Earth?"

"Only what I could prove: that we have a Colonial escort to see us safely into orbit."

"Didn't they think that was odd, considering that the last communication you sent, before the battle, was to the effect that the *Marabou* was under attack by Colonials?"

"They're talking about renegade Colonials, to cover that."

I sighed. "How much do the passengers know?"

"About as much as we know. They got a running commentary throughout, remember?"

"Well, it'll give them something to think about, anyway."

"More than that. Board Adviser Brown is launching a full-scale investigation."

I grinned. "That might shake a few assumptions."

"It'll shake more than that," he said grimly. "And speaking of shaking, what's this I hear about you shaking down the Company by holding the *Marabou* hostage?"

"I'm sorry they wouldn't give you a Falcon," I said.

"You mean you really did it?"

"Did what?" I was looking under the bed for slippers.

"Held the *Marabou* hostage? And strongarmed the Company?"

"Well, sort of. That is, nobody seemed to mind being taken hostage. Have you seen any slippers around here? In fact, hardly anybody even knew about being held hostage. And as for the Company, well, don't you think you warrant something more than standard hazardous duty pay for this mission?"

"What did you ask for? Besides the Falcon?" His eyes were an unreadable cold blue, distant and as unfamiliar as if we were strangers.

"Don't tell me you're angry with me," I said.

"What did you ask for?"

I told him.

Collis, who had been listening to all this in silence, brightened visibly. "You mean I'll be able to go in freefall with Papa? You'll find a med-tech who can fix my ears?"

"If it can be done, kid, you'll have it."

"Oh, Skyrider, thanks!" He hugged me.

Jamin frowned. "You knew I wouldn't back you up on this."

"I knew you weren't in any condition to object." I released Collis and looked at his father. "And that's the whole point. You two cannot share an environment, as it is. And you try, anyway. Maybe that's okay now, in peacetime, while the powers that be give you free access to gravity environments. But what were you planning to do if war broke out?"

He didn't try to pretend he hadn't thought of it. "We managed, before. We'd have found a way."

"Well, all I've done is find it for you. I hope."

He thought about it, and finally grinned. "Your slippers are under the bedside table." He pointed, and waited while I fished them out and put them on. When I looked at him, he was still grinning. "Some steely-nerved hotshot rebel you are. Legend has it you don't give a damn for anyone but yourself. What happened to that?"

"Not a thing. If the war comes, and I expect it will, I'll want competent pilots on my side. And I won't want them distracted by family problems, like where to keep their Grounder kids. When you're covering my ass, I want your full attention."

He made a parody of leering at me. "You'll have it."

"That wasn't what I meant," I said, embarrassed.

"Wasn't it, hotshot?"

"What wasn't?" asked Collis. "Will I get to go to war, too?"

"*Get* to!" said Jamin.

"Well, maybe," I said.

Both of them looked at me. I just smiled.

"War isn't exactly something you *get* to go to," said Jamin.

"I'm hungry," said Collis.

"Me, too," I said.

He gave in gracefully. "Just what I needed. Two hungry hotshots. The med-techs say you're free to go whenever you like. Feel up to facing the mess hall?"

"Why wouldn't I?"

"Do you realize how many members of the crew and passengers are waiting to congratulate you?"

"Oh. Well. There's a dispenser in my quarters. Let's go there."

"Why?" asked Collis.

"There's a lot you still have to learn about being a hotshot," I told him. "Rule number one: hotshots don't sign autographs."

"I saw you signing one, before," he said.

"Rule number two: nobody's perfect."

HARRY HARRISON

Buy them at your local bookstore or use this handy coupon:
Clip and mail this page with your order

TOR BOOKS—Reader Service Dept.
P.O. Box 690, Rockville Centre, N.Y. 11571

Please send me the book(s) I have checked above. I am enclosing
$_____ (please add $1.00 to cover postage and handling).
Send check or money order only—no cash or C.O.D.'s.

Mr./Mrs./Miss _____

Address _____

City _____ State/Zip _____

Please allow six weeks for delivery. Prices subject to change without
notice.

FRED SABERHAGEN

- [ ] 48520-4 THE BERSERKER WARS $2.95

- [ ] 48568-9 A CENTURY OF PROGRESS $2.95

- [ ] 48539-5 COILS (with Roger Zelazny) $2.95

- [ ] 48564-6 THE EARTH DESCENDED $2.95

- [ ] 55298-9 THE FIRST BOOK OF SWORDS $2.95
  55299-7   Canada $3.50

- [ ] 55303-9 THE THIRD BOOK OF SWORDS (trade) $7.95
  55304-7   Canada $8.95

Buy them at your local bookstore or use this handy coupon:
Clip and mail this page with your order

TOR BOOKS—Reader Service Dept.
P.O. Box 690, Rockville Centre, N.Y. 11571

**Please send me the book(s) I have checked above. I am enclosing
$_____ (please add $1.00 to cover postage and handling).
Send check or money order only—no cash or C.O.D.'s.**

Mr./Mrs./Miss _____

Address _____

City _____ State/Zip _____

**Please allow six weeks for delivery. Prices subject to change without
notice.**